"This'll get your motor humming." Karla slid a coffee mug in front of Dylan.

"Go on, try it." Her eyes were wide and persuasive.

Dylan took a sizable gulp. "Wow," he said after a long pause. "That is…really…"

He set the cup back down on the counter and pushed it back toward her, smiling.

"…awful."

Karla laughed. "Wow, don't hold back on my account, Captain McDonald."

"Maybe leave this one off the Coffee Catch menu."

"Coward!" she playfully called as she snatched back the full mug.

"Purist," he corrected. And just because her pout was so disarming, he added, "but the Captain part? You can keep that. How about you just give me a regular coffee today."

"Aye, aye, sir. One boring regular coffee, coming up." With a mile-wide smirk, she scribbled on the check before placing it facedown in front of him. "On the house."

Smiling, Dylan turned the check to face him. *Kaptain Koffee* was written in an artistic hand, with a little doodle of fish and bubbles running up the side so the "$0" was the last of the bubbles.

Karla Kennedy sure knew how to bait a hook.

ALLIE PLEITER

Enthusiastic but slightly untidy mother of two, RITA® Award finalist Allie Pleiter writes both fiction and nonfiction. An avid knitter and unreformed chocoholic, she spends her days writing books, drinking coffee and finding new ways to avoid housework. Allie grew up in Connecticut, holds a BS in speech from Northwestern University and spent fifteen years in the field of professional fund-raising. She lives with her husband, children and a Havanese dog named Bella in the suburbs of Chicago, Illinois.

Small-Town Fireman

Allie Pleiter

Recycling programs for this product may not exist in your area.

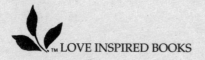 ™ LOVE INSPIRED BOOKS

ISBN-13: 978-0-373-81811-2

Small-Town Fireman

www.Harlequin.com

Printed in U.S.A.

In their hearts humans plan their course,
but the Lord establishes their steps.
—*Proverbs* 16:9

To Les, who never made me bait a hook

Chapter One

Coffee, doughnut. Coffee, doughnut. Coffee, Danish. Tea, toast. *Exile.*

Karla Kennedy ignored the ache of longing in her gut as she passed by the unused espresso machine to fill yet another basket of everyday coffee grounds for the ordinary brewer. Bringing an espresso machine to Gordon Falls—even the spectacular one Grandpa Karl had bought her as a graduation present—was an exercise in futility. Since her arrival last week, she'd only used the machine for one customer other than herself: a teenager who wouldn't know a well-pulled latte from a diner milk shake. Everybody else seemed to find the drinks overpriced and unnecessary, preferring the regular brew in Karl's clunky white mugs.

No one seemed willing to even try something new and refined—pure exile indeed for a foodie like herself. She might as well just give up and start subsisting on potato chips and Pop-Tarts.

A customer was here. All through culinary school, Karla knew she possessed the intuition Grandpa had told her about—the sixth sense that let her know a customer had come up to the counter needing something. "Shop eyes," Grandpa called it. Sliding the basket of coffee grounds into its place for the hundredth time on the commercial coffee machine, Karla turned and forced the weariness out of her voice before asking, "What'll it be?"

"Well, what do you recommend?" If his cobalt-blue eyes weren't enough to startle her, his question did the rest.

She couldn't help herself. "A trip back down the interstate toward civilization?" Feeling guilty, she amended to "Or the Tuesday special—coffee and…"

"Two doughnuts," the guy finished for her. "Pretty popular, I see."

"A Karl's Koffee Klassic." Some days Grandpa's fondness for *K*-based alliteration was a bit hard to take. She wanted to love the hokey charm of this place as much as everyone else seemed to, but it just wasn't coming.

"Myself, I've never been one for what

everyone else is having." Mr. Blue Eyes leaned against the counter, swiping off a baseball cap to reveal a mess of reddish-brown hair. Karla was pretty sure he was one of the firefighters from across the street who made up the shop's regular customer base, but without the usual Gordon Falls Volunteer Fire Department blue T-shirt, she couldn't be sure.

So he didn't want what everyone else was having? The espresso machine practically called to Karla from behind the counter. She felt a smile light up her eyes. If she could win over just one of those guys… "Well, you know, we're trying out some espresso drinks if you're interested in something different."

He looked intrigued, peering behind her at the mass of spouts and knobs. "Fancy. Karl's moving up in the world. How is the poor guy anyway? A broken hip takes a long comeback, I hear."

"Grandpa's doing okay." Karla wiped her hands on a dish towel and reached for one of the new cups and saucers she'd brought to the shop out of sheer desperate optimism last week. The standard-issue stoneware mugs everyone used for coffee in this place had to be twenty years old by her guess. "Three more weeks of physical therapy and he ought to be out and about."

"You're Karla," the man said, a disarming smile brightening his features. "Karl said he was getting you to take over while he was laid up." He slid onto the counter seat with an athletic grace. "Karla with a *K*, has to be."

It was a phrase Karla said over and over whenever giving her name to anyone. "That's me." Some days the *K* spelling was unique and helped people remember her. Other days it confused clerks and was just plain annoying. Another *K*-based alliteration; Grandpa Karl, Dad Kurt, daughter Karla. Sure, it proved useful for identifying junk mail and making small talk with bank tellers, but outside of Karl's Koffee it didn't hold much weight.

The customer unzipped his sweatshirt and stuffed the cap into the back pocket of his jeans. The open sweatshirt revealed a well-worn fire department T-shirt stretched across a broad muscular chest. The scent of early morning and river wafted across the counter—a wet, woodsy smell that never ceased to remind Karla of childhood fishing trips. Whoever this guy was, when he wasn't a fireman he was outdoors and active. He rubbed his hands together as if he found the coffee prospect as exciting as she did. "Okay, Karla with a *K*, what should I have this morning?"

Finally, a tiny bit of creative license! It was

like opening a window to clear a stale room. Karla carefully set the cup and saucer on the table between them. This was what she did best, what got her up in the morning. What filled the margins of her culinary school textbooks with ideas for adventurous menus and exotic flavor combinations. What made her similar to Grandpa but altogether different from him, as well. "Tell me your three favorite foods."

He raised his eyebrows, then steepled his hands together in thought. Karla's spine began to hum and tingle. The three other times she'd tried this favorite strategy to create the right coffee drink for someone, they'd huffed as if she'd handed them a final exam, and then ordered plain java. But here was a guy who got what she was trying to do. Who looked as if he found the process intriguing. After an electric moment of deep consideration, he replied, "Your grandfather's apple pie, a perfect steak and Dellio's fries."

The local diner's legendary fries didn't provide much of a clue, nor did the steak—except that he was a standard-issue Midwestern male—but the apple pie offered up a hint. "Cinnamon latte with an apple Danish."

She waited for his nose to turn up. For a fancy-schmancy coffee wisecrack to come.

Instead, he smiled. "I'm game. I've always liked my coffee strong and sweet anyways, and I am partial to a good Danish."

"Great." Karla grinned in victory, pulling the milk out of the small fridge below the counter. She launched into small talk while she worked the machine, just the way she'd been trained at the coffee shop back in Chicago where she'd worked her way through culinary school. Where she'd been one of the shop's best baristas. Where she'd solidified her calling to give interesting people exceptional coffee. "What's your name?"

"Dylan McDonald."

Now the river scents made sense. "The fishing guy?" Grandpa had mentioned that someone with that last name had started running fishing charters up the Gordon River for the tourist season.

"That's me. I've been up since four—this better have a good kick to it."

The day was looking up. "Kick starts with a *K*." Maybe there was a little more of Grandpa in her than she was ready to admit.

"Ha, that's a good one. You're a natural. How long are you in from the city?"

Karla tamped the finely ground coffee into the special container and slid it into the machine. "Shows that much, huh?"

"Well, the crack about the interstate was a dead giveaway. That and the fancy apron."

Karla smoothed a hand over the vintage apron that had been a graduation gift from her roommate. She'd started a collection during her last year of school while the dreams of opening her own shop started to really take shape. Wearing the distinct aprons to work in Karl's had been her declaration of sorts— no matter how many broad hints Grandpa dropped—that this stint was just temporary, not a gateway to joining the family business. "Oh. Well, I'm here until August or until Grandpa's back on his feet, whichever comes first." It wasn't that she didn't love her grandfather—it had been an easy decision to shelve her professional plans for a few months while he recuperated. It was just that no one seemed to realize she didn't belong here in Gordon Falls.

She certainly couldn't leave running Karl's to Dad. The "shop eyes" had skipped a generation in her family—Mom and Dad weren't up to running the coffee shop even if they did come in from two towns over to help out with Grandpa's recuperation. When the woman who rented the furnished apartment upstairs—where Grandpa and Grandma had lived back when they first opened Karl's—

was leaving for three months, it seemed as if God was ironing out all the details. The flat gave her a place to live above the coffee shop and not be holed up at home with her parents and grandfather. She had big plans to finalize—a girl needed her space, and Grandpa could be a handful.

"He's a good guy, your grandfather. He's been nice to everyone at the fire department for that matter. We all wish him well—you tell him that."

That confirmed Dylan was a fireman. The department was so close that those guys made up a huge portion of Grandpa's business. If she could sway even one of them toward an espresso drink, others would surely follow. The only trouble was that Grandpa was in the habit of plying the department with free coffee and doughnuts. Karla had taken enough restaurant management classes to know she ought not to be giving away free lattes and scones.

Only, that's how Grandpa conducted business. He seemed to always be giving away a lot of food. People loved him; could she really fault him for that? The shop was always packed with customers, and he took a personal interest in each one of them. "I'll tell him you sent good wishes. Here…" She placed the latte in front of him. "Tell me what you think."

Watching customers eat—or drink—something she made was one of Karla's greatest pleasures. Urbanites took their coffee beverages very seriously; it was a badge of honor when she got it right. People remembered and came back when she was on shift, so she learned the preferences of the "regulars." Here in Gordon Falls, however, folks didn't seem to be nearly so picky. Coffee was just that hot stuff that went with pie and…heaven help her…doughnuts. Needing a bit of an ego boost, and yes, not feeling it too much of a sacrifice to stare at the fireman's handsome face, Karla leaned on the counter and waited.

Dylan inhaled the aroma, catching the tang of cinnamon that now hung in the air. He wasn't going to gulp it down like so many of the Karl's Koffee customers—or "Klientele," as Grandpa liked to joke. He was going to enjoy it. Karla hadn't realized how much she missed genuine caffeinated appreciation until she watched Dylan's eyes warm with approval on the first taste.

"Good call." He nodded, indulging in a second sip. "I really like this. Not too sweet, but good and strong. Just waiting for a Danish."

"Oh, the Danish!" Karla had completely—and uncharacteristically—forgotten about the Danish. She hurried to lift the lid on the footed display plate so much that the glass clattered and a dozen people looked up from their ordinary breakfasts. "Gimme a sec to heat that up." She willed a flush to stay off her cheeks in the twenty seconds it took the microwave to warm the pastry.

"I got time," Dylan offered, a bit of latte foam lingering on the sandy stubble at the corner of his mouth. "Boat's back in and I don't have a shift at the firehouse for another six hours. All I have ahead of me is a lot of tiresome cleaning and advertising."

He said the last word as if it were a scourge. Marketing had been one of her favorite classes in school. She cocked her head to one side as she set the pastry in front of Dylan. "Advertising?"

He sighed. "I'm a great fisherman, but I'm no hotshot at publicity. I'm meeting with somebody from the state tourism board in an hour to see how Gordon River Fishing Charters can—" he made irritated quotation marks in the air with his fingers "—reel in a few more customers."

"You need to find a boatload of novice fishermen with deep pockets, huh?"

He narrowed one eye. "You say that like it's *fun*."

Wasn't it? She had a whole binder of marketing ideas upstairs on her kitchen table. Her shop would have great publicity. "PR's like fishing. You have to go where the fish are and offer the right bait. You should be good at it."

He took a bite of the pastry, momentarily closing his eyes to savor the Danish. Grandpa got his baked goods from a little German farm woman just down the river, who delivered fresh every morning. Karla was having trouble keeping her jeans from getting too tight given the quality of the goodies, even if she did prefer scones to doughnuts.

"I'd rather gut fish than advertise," Dylan admitted. "And I don't enjoy gutting fish."

"Yeah, but it's part of the job if you want to grow your business, right?"

"I prefer the term *necessary evil*."

Like coffee and doughnuts, Karla thought. Just to prove her point, two men at the corner table held their mugs aloft to cue her for a refill. "Be right back," she sighed, lifting the pair of glass carafes from their perches on the brewer and preparing for another tour around the tables.

Karl Kennedy's granddaughter didn't belong in Gordon Falls. Dylan couldn't claim to be an astute judge of female character—Yvonne had taught him just how wrong he could be about women—but Karla with a *K* clearly considered herself out of place in the quaint little tourist town he loved. Oh, she resembled her grandfather, but that was where the connection stopped. She was city all the way—from sleek dark hair that framed wide, ink-blue eyes to the boutique clothes and the manicured nails. She looked smart. As a matter of fact, she appeared highly ambitious. It wasn't a trait he valued much anymore. Still, the coffee was a welcome change—he'd all but forgotten the pleasure of fancy espresso drinks.

"I should have asked for your recommendation earlier," he said when she returned to the counter. "All those weeks of ordinary coffee…"

Karla chuckled, a low, sophisticated sound that pushed up one reluctant corner of her mouth. She wore an elegant shade of lipstick that he could only imagine came from some fancy city department store. "You must not come in here a lot."

It was true. Most days he was still out on the water at this hour, just finishing up with whatever junket of tourist fishermen he'd taken out on the river. He maybe came into Karl's once a week, if that. Based on what he was sipping, that might have to change.

"You're right. I'm just in early for my meeting." He took another long, slow sip of coffee. "Pity I can't put one of those machines on my boat—the last batch of investment bankers I had out were all complaining about having to forgo their usual grande-soy-mocha-whatevers."

"Not the supermarket coffee from a thermos type of guys, huh?" She raised an elegantly arched eyebrow.

Dylan winced at the thought of the can of supermarket coffee grounds in his kitchen and the dented old thermos currently rolling around the passenger seat of his truck in the parking lot. "This is exceptional coffee," he admitted. "If you ask me, a lot of that other stuff is just high-priced hype."

"Well, lots of it is."

"Not this."

She planted her elbows on the counter,

pleased at the compliment. "No, sir, not my coffee."

Dylan stared down at his cup, now nearly empty. He considered asking for another. The lady really did make a mean coffee. He took another sip. He'd never have thought to put cinnamon in there. And what had made him consent to one of those fancy drinks now that he'd retooled his tastes back to "black, one sugar" java? "You can make these to go?" Karl's never really did a "to go" business, but she looked ready to try new things.

"Absolutely. I mean, a couple of national chains have built a fortune on it—why not Karl's?" She shrugged. "Gordon Falls is just catching on. Or catching up."

There it was, that ever-so-slightly judgmental tone he'd see every now and then from charter customers. *Nice place to visit but I wouldn't want to live all the way out here.* It didn't take a marketing genius to see she wasn't terribly thrilled to be here. Which was funny to him, because Dylan had moved heaven and earth to be here. "Gordon Falls has lots of other charms."

"Yeah." She clearly didn't hold to that theory. He could spot that bored look a mile off.

Well, Chicago had bored *him*. Wouldn't she be surprised to discover he'd been one of those blue-suited, briefcase-toting caffeine junkies rushing to make the seven-ten downtown? He'd bought into the whole upwardly mobile mind-set, working long hours and hitting all the right societal notes. He'd even found himself the perfect partner in Yvonne, sure she was the love of his life.

Then the *love of his life* left him high and dry for someone with what she deemed were faster prospects for success. Ditch your future fiancé for his boss? Who did that? How had he not seen that icy vein of ambition in her before she'd slit it open right in front of him?

He could almost be thankful. Almost. With the life sucked out of him like that, it had only taken Dylan three weeks after Yvonne's grand exit to realize how much he had bought into a giant lie. He hated corporations. And suits. And cubicles in high-rise buildings. He'd never truly wanted any of it, just thought it was what he was supposed to want. Half of what he'd done, he'd only done out of Yvonne's urging for what he ought to be.

Startled out of his corporate stupor, Dylan woke up to what made him truly happy. He slogged it out six more months in that suffocating office to scrape together the boat, the money and the contacts to kiss Chicago goodbye and launch his charter fishing business.

He hadn't ventured the three hours back to Chicago since. He owned one suit for weddings and funerals, and hoped to never touch another briefcase again. The fancy coffee, however…that might be worth revisiting.

"I don't think I've seen you before," Karla remarked, straightening up off the counter. "What time do you normally come in?"

"I'm not much of a regular, and if I do get here it's rarely before ten-thirty."

"Well, that explains it. I'm usually done by eleven."

"Are you the only one who makes these?" He was pretty sure he knew the answer. Emily, the other server, was a nice enough lady, but he doubted the fifty-year-old ex-librarian cared to learn barista skills.

She smirked. "Let's just say I don't think you'd want Emily's version of a cappuccino."

He nodded in agreement.

"Karla?" someone called from the room full of tables behind him.

With the tiniest glimpse of weariness, she grabbed the glass carafe again from the brewer behind her and walked toward the sea of customers. Dylan took another exquisite sip and watched her move through the tables, efficient but not engaged, feeling his curiosity rise and stretch like a lazy cat. Or was that caution getting his back up?

Karla returned. "So…what brought you in today?"

"That tourism meeting." He checked his watch. It was only ten minutes until his meeting with Cindi the tourism rep—Cindi with an *i*, for crying out loud, with a flighty personality to match the alternative spelling. If he wasn't eager to go before, now he felt certain Cindi was too young, too perky and too cheerful to come up with anything truly effective. "Like I said, I need some new ideas to grow my charter fishing business." He'd gone through his savings faster than he'd expected launching this business, and pretty soon the boat loan payments were going to start becoming a challenge if things didn't pick up.

"What about applying a little added value? You could bring your customers in here. End their experience with a nice, home-style breakfast and some killer coffee."

While Dylan abhorred business school buzz-terms like "added value," the simple idea sounded ten times better than the unimaginative set of bullet points Cindi had emailed to him yesterday. "You know, it'd be nice to end the morning on a high note even if the customers came in empty-handed. Only I can't exactly pull the boat up to Tyler Street, you know?" Karl's Koffee sat right in the middle of Gordon Falls' main thoroughfare, Tyler Street. The shop was, in many ways, the social center of the town—at least for the locals. Tourists tended to breakfast at their inns or the more upscale restaurants.

Karla pulled a ballpoint pen from her apron pocket and a napkin from the canister on the counter. "Solvable..." One eye narrowed while she began making calculations, rapidly scratching numbers on the napkin.

"Hey, coffee here?" a call came from a table to his left.

Without looking up from her calculations, Karla held up one finger, "In a second..."

A disgruntled sigh from the customer made Dylan wince, then let out a breath as Karla circled a number at the bottom of the napkin. She slapped down the pen, reached behind her to the coffee brewer—again, almost without looking—and then stared at Dylan. "Stay," she commanded with a pointed finger just before dashing out toward the diners.

Woof, Dylan thought, annoyed. *What am I, a puppy?*

Still, he did stay. He told himself it was to finish off the great coffee, but the command still stung. Today's charter had been hard to take—a herd of accountants bent on upstaging one another the entire morning. As much as he chafed from the upscale customers, they were essential to his business. These past ten minutes had been the most pleasant of his day: it was nice to have someone take his satisfaction into consideration instead of the constant press of "customer service."

Returning, Karla slid the carafe onto the brewer so fast it nearly sloshed out the top. She had energy to spare, this woman. Eyes bright, she spun the napkin to face him. "How many trips do you have the rest of this month?"

Dylan squinted in thought. "Eight." That hurt to admit; it needed to be more like ten or twelve.

"Easy deal. You pay a flat eight dollars a head, I take orders in advance that you phone in from the dock, and they have perfect specialty drinks and such waiting for them when they arrive. That's if Grandpa approves it—" she parked her hand on her hip with an air of determination "—which he will."

Dylan had to admit, it solved a multitude of problems. His customers got a good send-off no matter what they caught—or failed to catch. If he was smart and applied himself, he could roust up some repeat business while they sipped. And good old Karl got some extra business. Maybe "added value" wasn't as evil as it sounded. "You're one sharp cookie, Karla Kennedy."

The corner of her mouth curled up into the cutest little grin. "Just for that, there's free lunch in it for you—well, late breakfast any-way—if you like."

Dylan liked that idea so much he ordered scrambled eggs and toast while he phoned Cindi to cancel their meeting.

Chapter Two

❧

"Looking good there, Grandpa!" Karla called to her grandfather and his physical therapist when she came in the front door of his house an hour later.

"That's what I told him," Rosa, the therapist, said, frustration clipping the edge of her words. Her grandfather was impatient and used to activity; ensuring that he got his rest was no small feat. The only thing harder than getting him to take it easy was coaxing him to do the required exercises to heal his hip. That lion-tamer of a job required patience, diplomacy and a thick skin. Medical progress aside, it seemed to irk Grandpa that Karl's Koffee was actually surviving without him behind the counter.

"We miss you at the shop," Karla confessed,

momentarily unsure if that would make it better or worse. "Everyone's asking how you are."

"How do they think I am?" Grandpa snorted. "I'm stuck using this stupid walker like some old coot."

Karla detoured into the living room to kiss her grandfather's cheek. "Yeah, but you're *my* old coot. It won't take long before you'll be kicking me out of here and running Karl's like always." That was a bit of an overstatement. While everyone agreed her grandfather would be back at his namesake shop sometime in the future, only Karl believed he'd be "running it like always." He'd needed to slow down even before the broken hip ground him to a halt.

Rosa raised one eyebrow while Grandpa merely growled. Evidently today's therapy session had been particularly prickly. Karla escaped to the kitchen, where she slid her handbag and a box of Danish from the shop onto the counter. Mom's tired eyes matched Rosa's as she looked up from the sink. Her parents, who lived twenty minutes west of Gordon Falls, were staying with Grandpa off and on until he could safely be on his own. The doctors thought that would be two more weeks. Grandpa thought it should be two more hours—hence Mom's weary expression.

"Everyone having fun today?" Karla teased.

"Oh, loads." With her father trying to keep regular hours at his shelving business during the day, Karla knew her mother's days with Grandpa could get long indeed. Mom nodded toward the living room, whispering, "Rosa is a saint. I'd have throttled him by now. If your father hadn't left an hour ago, I think they would have come to blows."

She knew the feeling. Kennedys—and those who married them—were doers. Action people, thinkers and planners. Grandpa's extended convalescence was taking its toll on everyone. Somehow, for reasons that weren't too hard to guess, all this was opening up an old Kennedy family wound. Karla's father, Kurt, had declined to take what Grandpa saw as his place behind the counter at Karl's. Dad's choice not to follow in his father's footsteps had always been a wedge between them. Karla's stepping in to run Karl's Koffee, even as reluctantly as she had, just seemed to drive that wedge an inch or two deeper. Add a painful surgery, long hours of fidgety Kennedys sitting around hospitals and living rooms, and combustion was unavoidable. Karla didn't opt to live in the apartment above the shop rather than here at Grandpa's house for no good reason—she'd leave that volatile situation to her parents, thank you very much.

"Your books came." Mom gestured toward the kitchen table. "Weighed a ton. I thought online classes didn't need all those textbooks." Karla had enrolled in an online restaurant management certificate program even before Karl's fall. Now she was doubly glad to have the business-related work keeping both her future plans in motion and her mind occupied while all the way out here in Gordon Falls.

Karla began opening the box. "I got a few extra books from the entrepreneurship program. Business stuff." Pulling off the packing tape, she removed the filling to see *Restaurant Ownership*, *The Chef's Guide to Marketing*, and *Culinary Management* alongside the two workbooks needed from her online courses. The used texts had clearly seen wear and tear, but they were half the price of the new ones. Plus, if she was fortunate, they came with highlights and notes from their previous student owners.

"Ambitious," Mom remarked from over Karla's shoulder. She lowered her voice. "Karl could probably tell you half of what's in those books." She winked. "Or so he'd boast."

"Aren't we done yet, Rosa? My hip is yelling at me." Grandpa's groaning echoed into the kitchen from the living room.

"A saint, I tell you." Mom was laughing,

but probably only because she was picking up her car keys. "I'm off to the grocery store. Do you need anything?"

Oh, there was a long list of what Karla needed, but Halverson's wasn't likely to carry any of it. "No, I'm going to place an order with the restaurant supply place this afternoon after I talk to Grandpa about something."

Mom raised a curious eyebrow. "You can tell me about it later, okay?" She ducked her head into the living room. "Karl, be nice to Rosa. She's here to help."

Karla heard her grandfather grumble something about the nature of helpfulness, punctuated by a yelp that generally signaled his descent into the recliner chair. His therapist walked into the kitchen, returning the blue cardboard folder that held the papers showing Grandpa's daily exercises to its spot on the counter. He was supposed to do exercises twice a day when Rosa wasn't here, but often refused. "Two more weeks." She sighed. "Remind him he can go out and about after two weeks but no driving for another month."

"We'll see about that!" Grandpa yelled from the living room. "Morehouse is a tyrant, I tell you."

Karla offered Rosa a shrug. "Dr. Morehouse

is on your side, Grandpa," she called into the other room. "Try to remember that."

"See if you can get him to keep his feet elevated with ice on that hip for twenty minutes twice this afternoon. After those exercise he *claims* he does, but doesn't." She looked at Karla. "I told your mom just what I told him—he's doing better than expected. He'll make a full recovery if we can just keep him from overdoing it."

Grandpa was the king of "overdoing it."

"I'll do my best. You take care. Want a Danish?"

Rosa sighed, took a Danish and headed out the door.

The minute the door closed, Grandpa was making noises in the living room. "Can we go out to lunch today? I won't tell a soul."

"Everyone will see you and rat you out." Karl Kennedy could no more walk down the streets of Gordon Falls unrecognized than Karla could whip up a soufflé over a candlestick. The man's coffee shop was the unofficial town hall. It was part of the charm—and the pain—of being here: everyone knew Karl, and everyone knew she was Karl's granddaughter. She was starting to really miss Chicago's anonymity.

"No one will tell on me. Call Vi. She'll

come spring me." Violet Sharpton had come to visit Grandpa multiple times in the hospital and stopped by every other day. While she was as feisty as Grandpa, Vi wasn't a likely conspirator for anything that would endanger his recovery.

"Dad would have my hide," she replied as she walked into the living room with a cheese Danish on a napkin. "You know that. And Mrs. Sharpton wants you to get better, so I doubt she'll help you cheat. We'll order out from Dellio's, how about that? Besides, I struck a deal at the coffee shop today and I want to tell you about it."

That got Grandpa's attention. "What kind of deal? You bringing in some other fancy machine no one knows how to work?"

It was true; no one else seemed to be able or willing to work the cappuccino machine. One high school student managed a brave attempt, but it ended in an incident so awful the entire shop staff had made a pact never to tell Karl how hazelnut syrup got into the heating vents. The other waitress, Emily, had nearly refused to touch the machine.

Karla sat down on an ottoman opposite her grandfather. "We're going to supply breakfast to Dylan McDonald's charter fishing customers once or twice a week. I worked out a package deal for the next month." She laid out the terms of the agreement as Grandpa ate the Danish. "We shook on it, but I told him it wasn't official until I got the okay from you."

"We're catering to McDonald's fishing boat?"

Grandpa's idea of catering would come something closer to a thermos of coffee and a box of doughnuts. "No, they'll place their espresso drink orders with Dylan as they pull into the dock and then I'll have it all set on a table when they walk in. Dylan will pay up front eight dollars a head. I figure some of them might end up staying and ordering a full breakfast if things go well." She smiled. "Everybody wins."

Grandpa grinned. "Well, look at you striking deals and making partners. Kennedys can do, I tell you." It was the unofficial Kennedy Family Motto. The old man winced and shifted, rubbing his hip. "McDonald. The fireman with the fishing boat business, right?"

"That's him."

Grandpa's gray eyes twinkled. "About your age, isn't he?"

She swatted her grandfather's good leg. "Nice try, old man." Age was the only thing she had in common with Dylan McDonald. Right now her focus was on her principal interest, not Prince Charming. She hoped one or two of the executives Dylan claimed to serve might prove useful business contacts. A woman on her way up in the world had to look for opportunities everywhere she could. If the deal with Dylan found her a commercial real estate broker, a potential investor, or just a handful of likely customers, she'd be thrilled.

As for the flannel-shirted, fine-looking fireman? She could always use a friend all the way out here, but she wasn't casting a line for anything more.

Dylan laughed to himself the next morning as he watched Karla continue her one-woman caffeine campaign. She was persistent, he'd give her that much. Violet Sharpton scrunched her face up after sipping whatever coffee Karla had put in front of her. "I thought you said there was chocolate in this."

"There is." Dylan saw Karla's face drop.

"Well, what else is in there messing everything up?"

"Espresso." Karla had to have known Violet was a tea drinker, didn't she? She wasn't that new to town. Still, the froth he saw on the edge of Violet's mug told him Karla had been trying out a new concoction on the old woman. Not that Violet wasn't a fan of new things—she was one of the most adventurous senior citizens Dylan had ever met—but some leaps were just a bit too far. "It's a strong, Italian kind of coffee."

Violet put the cup down. "I have teenage grandchildren—I know what espresso is. But I could have told you up front I'm not one of those caffeine junkies." She offered Karla a forgiving grin. "You're a sport for trying, though. Your grandfather could use a kick in the gastronomic pants once he comes back. Never tries anything new."

"Karl says he knows what people like," Dylan offered as he walked up to the counter.

"This 'people' don't much care for that." Violet nodded toward the brew.

"She made a pretty good latte for me yesterday." The remark returned a bit of the smile to Karla's face.

"Well, then, you youngsters go on ahead with your fancy drinks and leave the basics to the old folks." She put a hand on Karla's. "Nothing personal, hon, but I'll be glad when your grandfather's back up and running."

"We all will," Karla replied with a hint of weariness in her voice, making Dylan suspect Karl wasn't a model patient.

"Maybe I'll come by this afternoon. Bring him some homemade soup or such."

Karla took the cup and saucer back with an air of defeat. "He'd like that. He always perks up when you visit. No charge for the mocha, I'll just get you a tea. Milk and sugar?"

"Lots of both. Tell your mom I'll be by around three-thirty." Violet slid from the counter, standard stoneware mug in hand with a tea tag peeking out the top. "New ain't always better," she said before moving to a table filled with women her age.

He sat down where the old woman had been. "On a crusade?"

"I don't know why." Karla wiped off the counter in front of Dylan. "It's not like Grandpa's basic brew is bad or anything."

"You just have sophisticated tastes, that's all. I heard a group of the high school kids going on yesterday afternoon about there 'finally being decent lattes around here.' That has to count for something."

A little glow of pride brightened her cheeks. "No kidding?"

"No kidding." He produced an envelope with ninety-six dollars cash inside and placed it on the counter. "And here's the money to prove it. Next week's coffee catches, paid in advance."

Karla narrowed one eye. "Coffee catch?"

"I had to call it something. My sister came

up with it. A 'Coffee Catch' to round off your fishing trip."

"Please tell me you didn't spell it with a *K*."

He laughed at her obvious disdain for Karl's signature gimmick. "I suppose you're entitled to be tired of that."

"Like you wouldn't believe. Here, it's cute. But back in Chicago, it's all 'how do you spell your name again?'" She pulled in a deep breath as she slipped the envelope into the cash register. "Another cinnamon latte?"

"Nah. Surprise me again."

The look in her eyes was worth whatever drink came next, even if he had the same re-action as Violet had. She really liked doing this. "Sweet or salty?"

"Karla, check please," called someone from one of the front tables.

"Sure thing," she called back drily. "In a second."

"But I'm in a hurry." The whine in the cus-tomer's voice would have irritated anyone.

Karla shut her eyes. They were clearly running shorthanded without Karl—who had seemed to never leave the place—and it showed in the way she applied a smile as she pulled a stack of tickets from the pocket of her apron. "No problem, Mr. Sullivan. You'll be out of here in a flash."

"I'll hold my answer till you get back," Dylan said, watching her walk away. She seemed out of place, and yet oddly not. As if she was resisting any settling into the little town. It made sense: she had big ambitions written all over her, and Karl's Koffee was only a holiday spot for someone with those kinds of aspirations.

He spied an open backpack on the counter behind the cash register, and got a confirmation to his guess. *Culinary Management* was prerequisite reading for someone itching to get much further than waiting tables in Gordon Falls. Should it surprise him that someone as clever as Miss Kennedy had designs on moving up in the world? Ambition wasn't the root of every evil—he had to keep reminding himself of that. Not everyone on their way up stepped on anyone to get there. Still, her apparent drive made it easier to ignore her pretty eyes and engaging personality—once burned was enough for him.

"Well?"

Karla's voice pulled him from his thoughts. "Well, what?"

"Sweet or salty?"

He'd totally lost track of the question. "Um…both?" It was true, he didn't really have a preference. "Does it work that way, like sweet-and-sour pork?"

"Only sometimes." She squinted her eyes in thought, her fingertips drumming softly against the counter. "Are you willing to stray from coffee?"

He pulled back. "Like how?"

"Chai tea. A little spicy, but with milk and honey. Very global."

That was a joke. He plucked at the ripped sweatshirt he was wearing. "Dylan McDonald, international man of mystery?"

Her laugh was engaging, a musical sort of giggle, soft and light. "Yeah, you could say that."

"No offense, but it sounds like a girlie drink."

Now it was her turn to balk. "Tea? England's male population and half of the Middle East would take issue with your narrow-minded attitude, bub." That last word had a decided "I dare you," flavor to it.

Okay, he could have a little fun with this. "Fine. I am man enough to try chai whatever it is. But I'm not holding out a lot of hope here, and there had better be some serious caffeine in that cup."

She began working the dials on the espresso machine. "Oh, this'll get your motor humming. Maybe tomorrow I'll find some Japanese matcha. That's got more kick than most espressos." She leaned in. "And it's green. Kind of like algae."

"Now you're scaring me."

A few minutes later, Karla slid a tall mug in front of him. It did smell exotic, but not necessarily in a good way. Dylan was beginning to think this little game wasn't going to end well.

"Go on. Try it." Her eyes were wide and persuasive.

He took a sizable gulp. Closing his eyes, he took a moment to explore the many different tastes the drink combined. "Wow," he said after a considerable pause. "That is…really…"

Her eyes popped even wider and she leaned on the counter with both elbows.

"Awful." He set the cup down on the counter and pushed it back toward her.

"Oh, don't hold back on my account, Captain McDonald, tell me what you really think."

"I think it tastes like something fish would enjoy, not fishermen. Unless I'm hosting a fishing bridal shower, let's leave this one off the Coffee Catch menu. And the Machu Picchu algae? Let's skip it."

"Matcha," she corrected, then added a playful "coward," as she snatched back the full mug. The sparkle in her eye undercut any force she tried to give the barb.

"Purist," he corrected right back. "Tea's not my thing, never has been. If it's any consolation, I liked yesterday's contender much better." Just because her pout was so disarming, he added, "And the captain part. You can keep that."

"Aye, aye, sir. From now on, all beans, no leaves."

It took him a second to work out that she meant all coffee and no tea. "Steady as she goes. How about you just give me a regular coffee today—black, one sugar. You can surprise me again next Wednesday when I bring in the first customers."

"One boring regular coffee, coming up. On the house, on account of your recent culinary disappointment." She pulled one of the stoneware mugs from the shelf behind her, unceremoniously dumped in the sugar and filled it with coffee. With a mile-wide smirk, she scribbled for a second on a meal ticket before placing it facedown beside the mug in front of him and sauntered away to tend to a table.

Smiling, Dylan turned the check to face him. "Kaptain Koffee" was written in an artistic hand, with a little fish-and-bubbles doodle running up the side so that the "$0" was the last of the bubbles.

Karla Kennedy sure knew how to bait a hook.

Chapter Three

"And that's one half-decaf soy with extra cinnamon." Karla set the final beverage in front of Dylan's six fishermen as they sat at the coffee shop's front table the following Wednesday morning. Dylan had phoned in their orders fifteen minutes ago, and true to her expectations, each man had requested a highly specialized drink.

She was proud of herself; they might not ever have ventured into Karl's on their own, which meant her marketing idea had worked. Even at someplace as nondescript as Karl's, she had a knack for finding customers and giving them what they wanted. The affirmation bloomed a wonderful optimism in her chest. Grandpa always said skills were one thing and anyone could learn them, but the "sense" to run an eating establishment was an inborn gift. Today told her she had that gift.

Karla smiled to herself. The first official Coffee Catch was an odd sight indeed. While Dylan referred to them as fishermen and requested she do the same—evidently Kaptain Koffee had a knack for customer service even if he did hate marketing—Karla found that a generous term. Calling the collection of well-groomed men in front of her "fishermen" was like calling a guest at a dude ranch a "cowboy."

These six sure didn't fit any image Karla had of guys who normally cast hooks into water. All in their forties and dressed in upscale sportswear, this crowd looked as if they belonged on yachts at some oceanfront resort. She practically needed a calculator to add up the premium logos, brand names and expensive gadgets these guys touted. If they fished, it sure wasn't to put dinner on the table. Still, she was glad to have them in Karl's. These were exactly the type of customers she wanted to serve when she opened her own place.

A man in a sky-blue polo shirt and preppy plaid shorts arched his eyebrows after taking a sip of his double-shot latte. "Hey, this is good." Karla chose to ignore the surprise in his expression. *Hey,* she wanted to say, *you have not left the civilized world that far behind.* Which really was a case of the pot calling the kettle black—she'd had to drive forty minutes away to get all the supplies she needed to stock a full espresso bar and had been known to gripe about Gordon Falls' "overwhelming quaintness" entirely too often. Hadn't she just referred to her stint in Gordon Falls as "exile" last week?

"I told you I wasn't exaggerating," Dylan said, coming to her defense. His stained denim shirt looked especially ragged next to his current customers. His eyes were bright, even if his morning stubble gave him the scruffy, unkempt air. He smelled of soap and salt but still a bit of fish, as if he'd tried hard to clean up for his appearance in the shop but hadn't completely succeeded. He tucked his hands in his jeans pockets and glanced around the group. "Not a bad way to end a morning on the river, don't you think?"

"Makes up for the massive one that got away," Mr. Double Shot said, pushing his expensive sunglasses up on top of his head to give Karla a million-watt smile. Had she seen him on television? One of those trial lawyers with commercials and 1-800 numbers? He had that look of a man in search of his next deal. Dylan said they came from Chicago. Maybe he could be a future customer—lawyers liked power breakfasts, right?

"Now who's exaggerating," Half Decaf goaded. "I could have fit that fish in my pocket."

"Mixed luck out on the water?" Karla asked, setting a stack of menus in the center of the table. "Your coffee's part of the catch, but we'll whip up breakfast if you're in the mood for a bit more." She'd worked for ten minutes to come up with the perfect, nonintrusive way to hint that they might want to consider ordering breakfast.

"You cook as well as you pull a latte?" Double Shot asked, looking doubly charming as he extended a hand. "I'm James Shoemacher."

"Jim Shoe," Half Decaf cut in. "Call him Jim Shoe." He said it again, pronouncing it like "gym shoe" and pointing to his gleaming white leather sneakers just in case she didn't catch the joke. Shoemacher looked weary, as if years of repetition had rendered him immune to the gag.

The same way she'd grown wearily resigned to explaining, "No, that's Karla with a *K*" over and over. She shook Shoemacher's hand—one that didn't look like the kind that had done any time with night crawlers and a hook—and felt an unlikely kinship with the man. "Karla Kennedy." She nodded to the sign in the window. "Karl's my grandfather. And I don't do the cooking, but I can sure vouch for it."

"Shoemacher Realty. Industrial properties." Hmm...real estate. How fortunate was that? "And I've been up so long," he went on, "it feels like I ought to have lunch. Can you do a panini?"

"Sorry, no panini maker here, Mr. Shoemacher. We don't really do a lot of lunch fare." She almost laughed, picturing what Karl would think of the uppity term for a grilled sandwich. "But I'm sure I can set you up with a grilled cheese."

She expected him to grimace, but he smiled instead. "Do that," he replied. "But call me Jim."

As she pulled out her order pad, Karla decided she might have to eat her words about never making any business contacts in Gordon Falls. "Okay, one grilled cheese for Jim. Any of the rest of you need something more than your coffees?"

Half the group ordered a full breakfast, while three of them made a big show of checking their watches and smartphones, too busy to dally over eggs and toast.

"If you three need to head out, I'll go get

your cleaned catches wrapped up and iced for the trip home." Dylan had told Karla he was adding that extra service—and evidently it had been a good idea.

"Dave's will fit in his coffee cup, I bet," one of them snickered.

"Hey, at least I *caught* something," Dave replied. "So far all you caught was grief from your wife." That brought a laugh from the whole group.

"Dylan, we enjoyed our morning," pronounced Half Decaf, who had introduced himself as an accountant from a big firm Karla only barely recognized. "I'll have my assistant set us up for another later in the season." He sent a smile Karla's way. "And I'll be sure to leave time for breakfast."

Dylan shot Karla a grinning thumbs-up as he headed out the door with the exiting half of the group. So far, the first-ever Coffee Catch seemed to be a success.

"Dylan said this was your idea?" Jim asked when Karla brought their food orders to the table. At Grandpa's suggestion, Karla had asked Emily to come in a bit early so that Karla could give the fishermen her nearly undivided attention, only slipping out to make the all-too-occasional coffee drink for another customer. The executives seemed to enjoy the exclusive service—which had been the point all along.

"Seemed a nicer way to end an early morning than just getting back in the car," Karla replied. After a second, she quipped, "The espresso machine is too heavy to roll down to the dock."

"Smart and funny." Jim nodded to his two companions. "And all the way out here in the middle of nowhere."

"I'm from Chicago, actually," Karla explained. "Just finished culinary school. I'm helping my grandfather out while he's laid up from hip surgery."

"Culinary school. That explains a lot. So, Karla, what do you want to do after you finish helping Grandpa out?"

It seemed like a hundred years since anyone had asked her that question. Everyone in Gordon Falls only inquired how long she planned on staying—nobody seemed to care that she had shelved big plans to do time behind the counter. "I want to open a downtown breakfast eatery. A coffee shop like this, only a bit less..." She didn't know how to finish that sentence without seeming to put down her grandfather's beloved establishment.

"Rustic?" Jim finished for her.

Karla felt her face flush. "Well, yes." She

didn't want to insult Grandpa's place, just wanted to explain—especially to someone like him—that her dream had a lot more style and sophistication.

"It's a well-used real-estate term. Useful when explaining grilled cheese to the panini crowd."

She managed to laugh at that. "I get it."

"It's a very good grilled cheese," Jim added. "Takes me back, you know?"

"I'm glad you liked it." She looked at the other men. "Your breakfasts all okay?"

The other two nodded behind full mouths. "Hmm."

Jim pulled out his wallet and handed Karla one of those top-level charge cards. "I'll get this, boys." He also pulled out a business card. "When you get ready to open that place, Karla Kennedy, you give me a call. I'm good at spotting people who will go far in this world." He pointed at her. "You may just be the best catch of the day."

Karla slipped the business card in her pocket and smiled. She'd been moaning to God in her prayer journal last night that being cooped up in Gordon Falls was feeling like a colossal detour. This morning, however, felt like God's personalized reminder that she could pursue her dream even while out here. The card in her pocket—and the contact it represented—served as a deposit on the future she had beyond the counter at Karl's.

The massive tip Shoemacher added to the meager breakfast tab? Well that was very nice, as well.

"So." Jesse Sykes, a fellow volunteer fireman at the Gordon Falls Volunteer Fire Department, pulled on a gray T-shirt and shook his still-wet hair as they stood in the locker room later that afternoon. "How was the big rig gig?"

Dylan yawned—it was tiring to pull a shift as a volunteer firefighter right after a full morning of playing host to a bunch of city visitors. It was 3:00 p.m. and he'd been up for eleven hours already. "Not bad, actually."

Jesse took one last swipe at his hair before tossing the towel he held into the large canvas laundry bin in the corner. They'd just finished a demonstration at the high school, so it wasn't as if they'd just come in off a fire, but the heavy gear could make a guy sweat in January, much less June. "Today was the day you took them to Karl's afterward, right? How'd that go?"

"It's a nice perk—no pun intended." Dylan rubbed his own hair dry. "Puts just the right cap on the morning, especially if the fish haven't been biting, which they weren't this morning." One of the worst parts of the charter fishing business was that the satisfaction of his customers sometimes depended on the participation of Gordon Falls' finned inhabitants. This morning the fish had not been cooperative.

"Came in empty-handed?"

"Not completely, but there's always—" he made quotation marks with his fingers in the air "—the big one that got away." He laughed. "A lot of them got away this morning. Makes it hard to keep the customers happy, you know?"

"I can imagine." Jesse smirked. "Hey, I think the coffee thing's a pretty clever idea, actually. A way to add to the experience no matter how the fish are biting—and a bit more sophisticated than coffee in a thermos. Anything you can do to pull in the high-end crowd is always a good thing, right? You've got bills to pay."

Dylan shut his locker door and spun the lock. "Those boat loans don't care that I've just about run through my savings getting this thing up and running. As for the coffee, the whole thing was Karla Kennedy's idea, actually."

"Karla? Karl's granddaughter?"

"She's studying restaurant management, or something like that. I'd have never thought of it, being a 'coffee in the thermos' kind of guy." He smiled ruefully. "Although I did like whatever it was she made me the other day. Had cinnamon in it, and frothy milk. I gave up all that stuff when I stopped working downtown, but now I think maybe I might go back to some of it."

"So you talked shop with clever little Karla Kennedy." Jesse hoisted a bag over his shoulder. "There's brains behind those big blue eyes." He waggled one eyebrow at Dylan. "Reeling in more than the fishermen, are we?"

"She's not my type and I don't think I'm hers." Dylan leaned against the locker he'd just shut. "Karla's definitely a city girl. I get the feeling she can't get back to Chicago fast enough. You should have seen her charming up my customers—she definitely prefers a high-end kind of guy."

Jesse fished a watch out of his pocket and put it on. "You're a high-end kind of guy. You just do it in a down-home kind of way now."

"You just contradicted yourself, Sykes." Dylan sat down on the locker-room bench and began tightening the laces on his work boots.

"Not necessarily." Jesse tapped him on the shoulder. "Hey, wait a minute—I thought you told me this morning's fishermen were guys in their forties."

"They were." Dylan tied off the knot.

"So I highly doubt Karla was fishing for dates from them."

"I didn't say she was flirting with them."

"Maybe not with words." Jesse set his bag back down. "Look at you. You didn't even realize you were jealous."

"Cut it out, okay?" He was not jealous of the attention Karla had paid those businessmen.

"Likely she was just being nice. You know, making business contacts. You said she wants to open her own place back in Chicago, right?"

"She mentioned it a few dozen times."

"So she talked to you. A lot. And she made you coffee. And you said she gave you a free lunch the other day. Do the math here, buddy."

Dylan didn't even bother to reply. He only shot Jesse a glare as he stood up to go.

"Man, we have to get you out more. You're spending way too much time with fish instead of females."

Maybe I like it that way. "Ever since you started 'ring shopping' with Charlotte, you've become impossible, Sykes. Well, more impossible than usual." Jesse had been the firehouse's most proclaimed bachelor until a pretty, young Chicagoan named Charlotte Taylor had bought a property right out from underneath him. Jesse got himself hired to help Charlotte renovate that cottage, and it was safe to say the relationship had gone far beyond contractor-client since then. "You going to pop the question soon?"

Jesse's smile gave the answer even though he replied, "That, mister, is privileged information."

"Good for you. Really, I'm glad for you." He was—he and Jesse were good friends—it was just that the wave of happy couples in Gordon Falls was getting a little hard to bear. Starting with Fire Inspector Chad Owens, there had been four weddings and an engagement in recent years, and Jesse was about to make that number five.

Dylan hoped that would signal an end to the discussion, but no such luck. His buddy sat back down on the locker room bench. "Look, Dylan, you gotta put yourself back out there. You can't let Yvonne keep doing this to you—I can't stand to watch it. Just because she went after someone with deeper pockets doesn't mean every woman sees you as short on cash."

How many versions of this lecture was Sykes going to give him? Dylan glared at

Jesse again, hoping to signal his reluctance to hear any more on the topic.

"I mean it. You're doing fine for yourself. You are long on charm, buddy. Give yourself more credit. You're a catch. There are other fish in…"

Dylan rolled his eyes and held up one hand. "Stop with the fishing metaphors. Please, I'm begging you."

Jesse squared off at him. "Tell me you're over Yvonne."

"I am," Dylan declared as he bent down over his second boot, trying hard not to sound as annoyed as he felt.

Jesse shook his head and blew out a breath. "Nope. Make me believe it."

Dylan tied off his second boot so ferociously the lace broke. Determined to put an end to this once and for all, he stared hard at Jesse and growled, "I. Am. Over. Yvonne." He tried to remember that the other fireman had his best interest at heart. Still, no one could ever call Jesse Sykes subtle. For all his good-hearted companionship, the guy was an interpersonal bulldozer.

"And Karla Kennedy is…" Jesse circled his hand in the air, cuing Dylan to finish the sentence.

Just say what he wants to hear and he'll go

away. Dylan shrugged his shoulders. "Kind of cute and very smart."

"*Very* cute and *super* smart." Jesse pointed at Dylan. "C'mon, you said she dubbed you 'Captain'—that's a dead giveaway right there. The woman has eyes for you."

Of course it amused him that she'd begun to call him Captain, but he wasn't about to admit that to Sykes. The guy needed no encouragement. "I've sworn off women with hard-driving ambitions. Besides, she's going back to Chicago as soon as she can manage it."

"Maybe not, if you give her some good reasons to stay." Jesse slid his bag back onto his shoulder. "When's the next Coffee Catch thing?"

He almost didn't say, worried his pal would show up and do something everyone would regret. A talented tenor, Jesse had a regrettable habit of breaking into song at inappropriate times. "Next Tuesday."

Thankfully, Jesse turned toward the locker room door. But not before calling "More fat-walleted businessmen?" over his shoulder.

"Nuns."

Jesse spun around to stare wide-eyed at Jesse. "What?"

It was the truth, but Dylan immediately realized he should have made up something else.

Jesse would never let something like this go. "The sisters of Saint Cecilia's," he explained, applying his "don't get started" face. "They're on retreat. They booked a fishing expedition and evidently they like good coffee."

Jesse clapped his hands together, walking back toward Dylan. "Ha! Buddy, you're in. Nuns. They'll love you. Not a speck of competition in sight. It's a sign from above, I tell you." He laughed. "Fishing nuns. Only you, McDonald, only you."

Dylan felt compelled to defend the good sisters. "Hey, they sound like nice people. They'll probably be a lot less trouble than this morning's captains of industry, that's for sure. Those guys were high maintenance." He paused and blinked. "Can a guy be high maintenance?"

Jesse picked at the denim shirt Dylan had on. "It's not like *you'd* ever know."

Chapter Four

Karla wasn't surprised when Dylan showed up at her counter Thursday morning. He wore a wide smile, so it was safe to say he felt the Coffee Catch experiment had gone as well as she did. "What'll it be today, Captain?"

His eyes narrowed just a bit as his smile widened. "I have to say, that's growing on me." He wore a navy blue shirt that did splendid things with his tanned complexion, despite the fraying around the edges. The rugged attire definitely suited him, even if no one would ever call Dylan McDonald a clotheshorse.

"Oh, well—" she applied a mock scowl "—we can't have that, now, can we?" Karla turned the crank to shoot a burst of steam through the espresso machine, clearing out the piping for whatever Dylan would get this morning. "I was thinking hazelnut this morning. Less sweet, but smooth."

"Maybe a banana nut muffin to go with that?"

"Excellent choice." As Karla began making the drink, it struck her how much she'd been looking forward to Dylan's visit this morning. She was proud of her idea for the Coffee Catch, satisfied that it had worked out so well for everyone involved, including her. "So, who's coming Tuesday?"

Dylan got a funny look on his face. "Nuns."

"What?"

Dylan rolled his eyes. "Why is everyone so surprised that the sisters of Saint Cecilia's want to go fishing?"

He had a point. "I guess I shouldn't be. Lots of people like fishing, I suppose."

She'd said that wrong; his expression perked right up, catching the disdain she'd neglected to hide from her voice. "But not you."

Karla busied herself with the hazelnut syrup. "Well, no. It's not my favorite." As the words left her mouth, she realized just what she'd let herself in for. When she looked up from the mug she was filling, Dylan's hands were planted on his hips.

"I'm going to have to take offense at that.

Fishing is wonderful. This is Gordon Falls, after all. Fishing is practically our national pastime."

She poured the steamed milk into the mug to mix with the fragrant coffee. "I don't think a town can have a national pastime."

"Don't get technical. I know Karl fishes. You can't tell me your grandpa never took you fishing."

"Oh, he did. Lots of times. It was sort of fun when I was little." Why hadn't she had the sense not to get into this discussion with someone like Dylan?

"Then what made it not fun when you were bigger?"

There wasn't a safe way to answer that. There were times when peaceful afternoons out on the river made for good memories. It was just that as she grew up, those long stretches out on the water too often ended up in tense arguments between her father and grandpa. "It wasn't the fishing, so much as the fisher*men*." She slid the steaming mug toward him and lifted the dome off the glass plate where the muffins sat piled.

Dylan caught the plural. "Obnoxious brother?"

"Oh, no, I'm an only child of an only child. Let's just say Dad and Grandpa don't always paddle their boats in the same direction." That felt much kinder than the memories of arguments she'd tried hard to forget ever happened. Some of those trips were the first times she'd become aware of her difficult position between her father and grandfather. She loved them both, but most times they had such a difficult time loving each other. It was one of the reasons she'd consented to come out here when Grandpa needed help—leaving Dad and Grandpa alone with each other was always a dicey proposition.

"Oh."

She was glad Dylan seemed to catch on to what she was saying. This wasn't the kind of thing she wanted to relay in any detail.

"Water isn't always a peacemaker, is it?"

Funny thing was, it always had been for her. Even when the prospect of going out with Dad and Grandpa held the good chance of a fight, she went anyway. "I like the water. It's why I like Chicago. Back home, I get out to Lake Michigan whenever I can."

"The lake is nice, but I found it too big. Give me a river any day."

She looked at him curiously. "You used to live in Chicago?"

Something flashed behind his eyes before he answered. Chicago was evidently a sore subject. She watched him measure out his words the same way she'd just done. "It wasn't for me." There was a long story behind that short answer.

"So you came here."

Dylan took a sip of the coffee she'd made, nodding his approval. "Oh, I like this better than the last one. Maybe even better than the first one." He glanced at her for a long moment. "I should have come here all along, but I let other people convince me of what I wanted." Then he took another sip, a longer one, making Karla wonder if he was buying himself time to decide how much he was going to say. "Don't ever do that."

"I've got my own dreams clearly in sight." She patted the *Small Business Strategies* textbook where it sat on the counter. The look in his eyes made her add, "And now it looks like you do, too. Captain of your own destiny, as Grandpa would say." The "as if" expression on his face made her wonder if that was why he seemed pleased and annoyed at the "Captain" title. His fishing business meant much more than a paycheck to him, she could see that.

"I've poured everything into Gordon River Fishing Charters. It's going to work out because I'll do whatever it takes to make it work out." He turned up one corner of his mouth in a half smile, half grimace before adding, "Even marketing."

"I imagine you will," she replied. The determination in his eyes made that easy to believe.

Dylan took another sip and then set down his mug. "Are you working Saturday morning?"

"No, my dad takes over on Saturday mornings."

"Then that settles it. You're going fishing."

Karla let out a moan. "Don't you have a charter or something? Boy Scout field trip?"

"As a matter of fact, this is my only free Saturday this month. I think you need to go fishing."

"No, really—it's not my thing."

Dylan picked up the coffee mug again, hoisting it up in front of her face as if it were Exhibit A.

"You got three tries out of me. I think it's only fair I get three hours out of you. Five-thirty to eight-thirty Saturday morning."

"Five-thirty a.m.? You want me to get up at dawn on my day off?"

A playful grin crept across his face. "It's not like you won't have enough coffee."

"There isn't enough coffee *in the world*,"

she complained, leaning against the counter. "Is the sun even up then?"

"Just barely. It's the best time to be out on the river." He pointed to the *Commercial Baking* recipe book open on the back counter behind her "Besides, anyone who wants to be a baker ought to be ready to rise before the sun, right?"

"Let's see—" Karla looked up at the ceiling, squinting in mock consideration "—the smell of freshly baked bread greeting the sunrise, or the smell of fish? It's such a tough choice."

"Let's see," Dylan matched her tone, "standing in a cold, dark kitchen staring at an oven or the thrill of landing a prize fish in the glorious setting of a river at sunrise? It's such a *tough* choice."

"Hey, that sounds like marketing talk to me. What did you do before you came out here to launch your dream job?"

All the light left his handsome face. "I sat miserably doing nothing that really mattered."

"Ouch. Sorry to bring it up."

He ran a finger around the rim of the mug. "You couldn't have known. Most of the world hasn't caught on to the soul-killing nature of institutional cash-flow analysis."

Karla stared at him. "Wait...you had a corporate job?" She tried to imagine Dylan in a suit and tie, but couldn't.

"I'd rather not talk about it." He looked up. There was so much going on behind his eyes. "I'd rather take you fishing."

Her curiosity got the best of her. "Okay, three hours. I bring the coffee—you never bring the subject up again after Saturday. Deal?"

"Deal."

Dylan put his hand to the doorknob of the firehouse conference room Friday night like a man greeting his execution. Meetings. To his mind, there wasn't anything more joy crushing than a committee meeting. His aversion to meetings had been solidified back at his former office job, and Dylan wasn't in any hurry to build on it. If Chief Bradens hadn't personally asked him to serve on the firehouse's 150th Anniversary Committee, there wasn't a soul in Gordon Falls who could have made him be here. No soul except Violet Sharpton. Dylan couldn't rightly say if Bradens had sicced the feisty old woman on him, but Violet had nevertheless cornered him after Sunday services last week saying they "needed new brains in the room" and wouldn't take "no" for an answer. Chief Bradens on his own was a force to be reckoned with, but when tag-teamed with Violet Sharpton? Well, Dylan was smart enough to know when he was licked.

Lord, I don't mind telling you I'm in no mood for whatever lesson You have in store for me here. Death by committee isn't the way I'd choose to go.

The rectangular meeting room table was all filled except for one seat: his. Normally a pretty prompt guy, Dylan just couldn't bring himself to hustle to this meeting and as such was five minutes late. He'd happily have supported the firehouse's 150th anniversary any other way, and planned to jump on any opportunity to escape into a more task-oriented role. If only that didn't look like the slimmest of possibilities. Dylan was so absorbed in his exit strategy that he almost didn't register the biggest surprise in the room: Karla Kennedy sat between Vi and her grandfather.

He caught her gaze as he settled into his seat. She wore the same "what are you doing here?" look he must be wearing. If Dylan couldn't figure out why he was on this committee, he had even less of a clue why Karla was here. She wasn't even a Gordon Falls resident, nor did she profess any desire to stay in town once Karl had recuperated. Not to mention that next to Clark Bradens—who was the youngest fire chief Gordon Falls had ever hired and by definition had to be here—Dylan and Karla were almost a decade younger than anyone else in the room. So he and Karla constituted Violet's "new brains"?

He took a moment to survey his fellow committee members. Chief Bradens's father and predecessor, George Bradens, was to his left. George was a friendly, caring guy—an honorary dad to half the department and a pillar in the Gordon Falls community. Next over sat Pastor Allen from the church. Dylan liked the man—he was compassionate without meddling and easy to talk to. Next to Allen sat Margot Thomas, the high school principal.

At the head of the table opposite Chief Bradens sat Ted Boston, the round, slightly self-aggrandizing man who'd been mayor of Gordon Falls for as long as anyone could remember. According to the chief, this town-wide celebration had been Boston's idea. It made sense in some ways; the firehouse seemed to be the hub that held Gordon Falls together. It sat in the center of town in more ways than one, Chief liked to say. Next to Boston, Violet Sharpton sat smiling at Dylan, practically beaming in satisfaction. That couldn't end well, and knowing Violet, there was more to it than met the eye. Dylan felt the weight of suspicion settle in his stomach like a rock.

The usual formalities of introductions and basic goals went by without incident. Another boring, ineffective meeting like the hundreds he'd endured in his former life. The firehouse was important to him; he knew he ought to participate. But as it was, Dylan ended up devoting more energy to trying not to look at Karla than he did mustering up some enthusiasm for the celebration.

"I'll be honest, people," Mayor Boston said as he leaned back in his chair, "the last thing this town needs is another potluck dinner. I want us to come up with something unique, something that will really pop. Something to put Gordon Falls on the map."

It was one of Boston's favorite phrases; he was always talking about ways to put this town "on the map." Dylan thought Gordon Falls was holding its own rather nicely and didn't need much help in the public relations department. It was part of the reason why he'd come here.

Blank faces met Boston's challenge. *If you needed new ideas,* Dylan thought a bit sourly, *why'd you ask the same old people who run everything else in town? The same old people except for Karla and me, that is. And why* us? Dylan realized he wasn't being fair in his criticism, but his good mood had left the room a while ago.

"That's why I brought Karla," Karl pronounced, as if reading his thoughts. "She's a fountain of good ideas." He looked right at Dylan when he said it. Karla went a bit pale and looked down at her hands.

Dylan had to admit, Karl wasn't wrong there. "I have had a lot of success with the Coffee Catch she dreamed up," he offered, if only to take the blanched expression from her features. "But, Karl, you're bound to be fully on your feet long before July. Don't you think we ought to let Karla get back to her business in Chicago?"

"It's no good to rush these things," Violet cut in, her voice pleasant but with a decided edge. "Let's not go giving Karl any deadlines he can't meet. I like to think Karla can help bring a visitor's perspective. Besides, Karl can always help sitting down."

Karl *hurrumphed* at Violet's coddling. "Don't you worry about me, Vi."

"So, July is when you are planning on the event?" Karla piped up, obviously feeling the squeeze of being seated between Violet and her grandfather.

"The official anniversary date is July 15, but that's a Sunday," Chief Bradens answered. "Pastor Allen has already agreed that we'll honor the firefighters in church that day, but we were hoping to have some kind of special event on the Saturday before."

Karla looked as if that solved everything. "That's Bastille Day."

Befuddled expressions met her pronouncement. "What's that got to do with the firehouse?"

"Well, nothing directly," she replied, "but it does hand you an easy way to have a unique kind of celebration."

Dylan had spent enough summers in Chicago to see where she was headed with this. "The Venetian Night boat parade." It wasn't a bad idea at all.

"What?" Violet's smile was curious but a mile wide.

"Every July Chicago celebrates the weekend around Bastille Day with a boat parade," Karla answered to the entire room. "People decorate their boats with lights and streamers and all kinds of things, and then they have a sort of parade out on the water at night. It's beautiful."

"We've never done anything like that before here," Principal Thomas said. "It'd be an easy way to get all kinds of people from the community involved. Even the students."

"It's barely a month away—can we get it done in time?" Chief Bradens wondered aloud.

"I don't see why not. We could let each boat pick a decade from the one hundred and fifty years the firehouse has been in existence," Mayor Boston suggested as he looked up from taking furious notes.

"Or just let them use the color red. Or firemen in general. There are loads of ways to do this." Karla's entire expression had changed from suspicious boredom to genuine excitement. Until, that is, the moment when Mayor Boston turned to her with an authoritative gleam in his eye.

Oh, no. He knew that gleam. Chief Bradens had that gleam, too, and it only meant one thing. Poor Karla—she didn't know what she'd just done, did she? Her next month was a goner—if she was even planning to stay that long.

"Miss Kennedy, I think you've hit on a grand idea," the mayor said. "I think Gordon Falls will be in your debt after you've chaired such a marvelous celebration. And to think our young people will be the ones to spearhead this effort. It's a most exciting thing."

Dylan watched in sympathy as the shock registered on Karla's face. "But wait…I…"

"Of course she'll chair the thing," Karl piped up before Karla could even finish her objection. "But hang on—we can't expect her to do all this by herself."

"No one's asking her to," Violet replied. Dylan's gut dropped to the floor when Violet turned her sweetest gaze to him and said, "Ted said *young people*."

Mayor Boston turned his head slowly to look straight at Dylan. "I most certainly did."

"You don't…" Dylan sputtered, feeling inevitability rise up and swallow him like a high tide. "I mean…" He felt the next four weeks slip through his fingers as though Violet had personally yanked them from his grasp.

"I'll gladly free up Dylan's time so he can chair the event. It's a great idea." The chief had the good sense to look pleased that he'd just dodged the chairmanship himself.

Before another ten minutes went by, subcommittees for decorations, food and publicity had been formed, and Dylan found himself approving a weekly Thursday meeting for the next month. His peaceful, autonomous life had just evaporated right before his very eyes. He was supposed to be building a business, not running a parade. Surely he and Karla could find some way to get themselves out of this before it went any further. Because even if it was June, this was Gordon Falls—and this town was very good at letting things snowball out of control.

Chapter Five

Karla marched up to Dylan's truck while Grandpa slowly wheeled his walker out to the parking lot. Behind her he could hear the old man boasting about his "smart girl" to Pastor Allen. "What just happened in there?"

"We've been ambushed." Dylan shook his head. "This whole thing took me by surprise." He bent toward her and whispered, "Do you think they had that planned all along?"

Karla looked over at Violet, who was beaming at her grandfather. "I can't believe it, but I think they did. You and I seemed to be the only two in the room who didn't see this coming."

"Not exactly fair to you." She couldn't know what an uncontrollable beast a Gordon Falls committee could become. This bordered on entrapment.

"Not exactly fair to either of us." Karla ran a hand through her shiny dark hair. "And I walked right into it with my bright idea, didn't I? I'm sorry I ever opened my big mouth."

Dylan leaned up against the words *Gordon River Fishing Charters* painted on the side of his truck. He tucked his hands in his pockets. "Don't knock it… It is actually a good idea. But I'm with Ted—no one needs another potluck banquet around here." He shrugged. "Ambushed or not, it is a much better plan than anything they would have come up with. I do like it."

Karla leaned up against the truck beside him. "Enough for us to chair it?" She looked as if she might actually go through with it, but she was smart enough to realize this wouldn't just be a simple, fun, as-long-as-I'm-stuck-in-town-I-might-as-well-do-something project, didn't she?

He couldn't leave her high and dry. If she was going to stick with it, the least he could do was go along with it until they could figure out another plan. "Well, I certainly can't endorse the tactics."

"No, that was sneaky. I'm going to have to have a talk with Grandpa and Vi. But it wouldn't be so awful. There'd be just enough time to pull it off."

He'd walked into this parking lot determined to get her help to ditch this chairmanship. Now he was agreeing to stick with it? What happened to the whole "Captain of my own destiny" thing? It was like some other, vastly more foolish man had taken over his vocal cords as he looked into those pretty blue eyes and heard himself say, "I suppose I could see my way clear."

"At least it will give me something to do in this town. No offense, but I'm getting pretty bored around here."

That just showed how little she knew about what it was like to live in Gordon Falls. Sure, it seemed charming and rustic to a visitor. He'd come here himself to simplify his life. It was only lately that he'd come to realize how complicated it had become instead. And now this. He managed a dark laugh—at himself, mostly—as he checked his watch. "At the very least we can keep the meetings from becoming three hour gabfests. That thing went on way too long for me." He looked up pensively at the night sky. "I should probably mention my bone-deep revulsion of meetings."

"No kidding." Karla laughed in reply. "It showed all over your face."

He winced. "That obvious?"

"Let's just say that if anyone had any doubts

whether or not you came into this voluntarily, I think you put them to rest."

Dylan winced. "I really hate meetings."

"Well, you'd better tell Vi." Karla looked over at the older folk who were still grouped in animated conversation. "I'm surprised she's not taking a victory lap around the parking lot."

"With your grandfather," Dylan added. "He was having a lot of fun, too. Those two are up to something."

Karla sighed. "Actually, I think he's just glad to be out of the house for anything."

"That doesn't mean you have to chair a town-wide, last-minute boat parade." He wanted to give her one last chance to get out of this right now.

She shrugged. "Oh, I don't know. On the one hand I could throttle him for dragging me into this. Then again, I haven't seen Grandpa this happy in a while. He needs something to do and to take his mind off that hip, and I don't think he can do this without my help."

Dylan shifted to face her. "Gordon Falls is full of people who could step up to the plate to help Karl. People who live here, who owe something to the community. I'll stand up for you if you want to bail. I don't think it's really fair what they did to you."

"Oh, and leave all this on your shoulders? How fair would that be?"

Dylan looked over her head. The older folk were now sitting and talking on a bench beside the church parking lot as if they had all the time in the world. He had three more charter contracts to mail tonight and a stack of maintenance bills to pay. "What if we take the reins for a little while, do most of the heavy lifting to get it set up, then come up with some reason to hand it off to Karl and Vi. You heard how many ideas they had—I think they really want to do it themselves and we're just stand-ins."

It seemed like the best solution for everyone. The prospect of working with Karla for a little while wasn't exactly an unpleasant one. And if they were planning an exit strategy all along, it would make it easier to spend time with her because neither of them would be assuming things that weren't going to happen.

"We could work it so they don't know," Karla said. "Set it up so it looks like they're stepping in to save the day. Vi and Karl will look like heroes." She leaned back against the truck as she gazed over at her grandfather. "Look at his face. Grandpa needs a little time in the limelight, don't you think?"

Dylan realized he'd never asked. "Karl

does know you're going back to Chicago, doesn't he?"

Her silence was telling. "I've told him, but I think he's choosing not to hear it."

"Then won't you doing this just make it worse?"

"Actually, I think it will be an improvement. If we do this right, it'll be a much nicer finish line than 'whenever Grandpa feels better.' I'll spend the next three weeks setting up Gordon Falls' perfect summer event, time it so that something calls me back to Chicago by the beginning of July, and then let a rehabbed Grandpa swoop in and bask in the glory. I could even slip back into town just for that weekend and watch all our plans bloom into Grandpa's victory lap."

It felt convoluted and a bit over the top. Only, it also made a complicated, twisted sort of sense. At least he had an exit strategy they both agreed on, and no one could argue Karl and Violet didn't deserve their chance to look like heroes. He and Karla were just making that happen in a roundabout kind of way.

"Okay—" Dylan extended a hand "—we have a deal."

She took it and gave it an exaggerated shake. "Captain, indeed we do."

"By the way, Cocaptain," Dylan called as

she headed for her car, "we're still fishing tomorrow morning."

"I can hardly wait." Sarcasm dripped from her words.

"Think of it as our first executive planning session. Bring lots of coffee."

"Super strong and lots of it," she replied. "Five-thirty? Really?"

"Really."

"I don't know why I'm saying yes to this."

Dylan knew exactly how she felt.

Fatigue pushed down Karla's shoulders as she climbed the steps to her little apartment above the coffee shop. It was homey in a Gordon Falls kind of way, but it lacked the panache of her city loft. Dad and Grandpa had covered the loft's rent while she was here helping out, so she could look at this extended stay as a "family-rescue working vacation," at best, and a chance to work at something close to her chosen profession, at the very least.

Tonight she'd inadvertently turned it into something else besides. *What made me suggest that event?* she asked herself as she turned the big, old-fashioned key in its pretty lock. *What have I gotten myself into now?* It wasn't as if there was much else to do in Gordon Falls when she wasn't at Karl's. It was pretty, but also pretty quiet. Downright boring, some nights. Sitting in Grandpa's living room watching loud television with Mom and Dad wasn't her brand of entertainment. At least the anniversary thing would give her something to occupy her time. She'd always had a knack for events, and her cochair wasn't so hard on the eyes, either.

Her cell phone rang just as she put down her bag. "Did you check your email yet?" Her Chicago roommate and fellow culinary school graduate Brenda Billings—or "Bebe" as almost everyone knew her—sounded incredibly excited. The pair had endured no end of "BB and KK's apartment" jokes since they moved in together at the start of their final year.

"No. You won't believe where I've been." Karla put Bebe on speaker and began scrolling down through her smartphone to see what email might have gotten her roommate all riled up.

"At a barn raising?"

"Very funny. No, at a committee meeting. Guess who's the new cochair of the firehouse anniversary committee?" She found an email from her favorite teacher at the school with an "Are you interested in this?" headline, noticing Bebe was also on the recipients list with a handful of other students. She tapped it to open up the email. "The message from Chef Daniel?"

"That's the one. So your grandpa's recuperating by running some charity shindig, huh? Sucked you into it, as well?"

Karla began reading. "You could say that..." The content of the email stopped her short. "Whoa...Bebe, is this for real? I thought Daniel said they weren't doing this at the Clifton anymore." The Clifton internship had been one of the best opportunities the school had to offer its graduates. In the past, the very posh Chicago hotel had taken a handful of culinary graduates on to the staff for year-long paid apprenticeships, but Chef Daniel had told the class the Clifton had stopped the program as of this year.

"It's down lower in the email. Evidently they changed their minds. We're *recommended*, Karla. I got the pastry spot in the kitchen and you got the spot at Perk." Perk was the Clifton's on-site coffee bar, and about as upscale as caffeine came in downtown Chicago.

"Wow. I mean really wow. A year getting paid to learn how Perk works before I open my own place? I can't believe it!"

"I know. I know!" Bebe nearly squealed. "I've been sitting here waiting for you to call and I couldn't stand it anymore so I called you. *The Clifton*, Karla. One month from today we'll be working there. I looked it up online. They have properties in Hawaii, Monaco, and Fiji." Bebe wanted to bake all over the world—well, mostly all the warm and pretty spots after enduring Chicago's harsh winters.

Karla opened her laptop to peruse the long email on a larger screen. Sure enough, the second paragraph from the bottom posted the position starting date as Monday, July 16. With a smirk, she cast her glance heavenward. *Cutting it a little close here, aren't we Lord? Still, thanks. This is a huge blessing.*

"Karla…"

"Sorry, I was just reading the whole email. I can't believe the Clifton program is back on and we're in."

"Reply right now. I mean it. Email Chef Daniel and tell him you're in. He knows you're out of town but you don't want him to give this gem to someone else."

She'd have to miss the firehouse event. Or leave right after the Sunday service that was supposed to end the ceremonial weekend. Or— She could figure that out later, for crying out loud. God had just handed her the perfect launch into her new life—the details could sort themselves out later.

"I'm going to hang up and reply right now. I'll read this over more carefully, too. I'm glad you called—I've got an early morning and I might have left my email until tomorrow if you hadn't tipped me off."

Bebe laughed. "Okay, you can tell me all about the town festi-whatever after you say yes to Daniel. Got the opening shift at your grandfather's tomorrow morning?"

Karla looked at her watch, declaring five-thirty way too early for someone likely to now lie awake all night pondering her future in exclusive coffee service. "Um…something like that. Hey, congratulations. We made it to the big time, huh?"

Karla could hear Bebe's wide smile in the tone of her words. "As big as it gets, Karla. We are on our way."

Chapter Six

Dylan watched Karla draw her sweatshirt closer around her. "Aren't there any fish on the river in the afternoon?" Considering what Karla Kennedy planned to do for a living, she didn't seem like much of a morning person.

"Sure there are." He slowed down the boat's motor so there wasn't so much misty morning breeze blowing in their faces. "But they're hiding and they're definitely not hungry. You want to fish, you have to get up early. Surely your grandpa taught you that."

Karla clutched her coffee thermos. "I remember predawn seeming a lot more inviting when I was eleven." Her halfhearted attempt at being cheerful was amusing in its ineffectiveness. Honestly, she looked as if she'd been up all night, but he didn't think that was ever a safe thing to ask a woman.

He chose to encourage her instead. "Oh, it's the best time of day in my opinion. The sun coming up over the river? That's pretty much the finest thing you'll ever see."

She narrowed one eye at him and sipped her coffee. "I would have been okay taking your word for it, you know."

Dylan ignored her slip into predawn grumpiness. She had his cell phone number so she could have declined his offer to go fishing even as late as this morning. No, she wasn't delighted to be here—well, not yet—but she was still here by her own choice. Give her the chance to land a great big fish in the fresh morning sunshine, and that sourpuss face would be long gone.

He pulled into his favorite spot; a bit of a cove just beyond the river's bend north of Gordon Falls. As the motor cut, the blissful quiet of the morning wrapped around the boat, broken only by the *plop* of the anchor hitting the water. Gentle, lazy waves lapped against the boat hull and carried a confetti of summer leaves past the bow. Karla yawned and stretched as a half dozen birds rustled the branches that spanned out over the current. Everything was shifting from gray to pink as it reached for the eastern sun. Nothing, *nothing* ever fed his soul like mornings out on the river.

"So this is your personal boat?"

He stepped down off the bow of the *Low Tide*. "The *High Tide*, the one I use for charter trips, is much bigger. I had this one first, even before I left Chicago. It took me six months to secure the loans and fix up the *High Tide* for charter work." He removed a pair of fishing poles from the long shelves that ran down the side of the boat. "I like having two boats—helps it not to feel like I'm at the office when I go out for myself, you know?"

"I get that."

Dylan flipped open a cargo lid and brought out a tackle box. "Did your family have a boat?"

"We had one, but it was tiny. Not as big as this and certainly not as big as the *High Tide*. The place downriver, where my grandfather used to live—where Dad grew up—had a long dock that went out into the river. We fished off that, too, but not as much."

Clearly, fishing was a mixed memory for her at best—he wanted to explore that, but even more he wanted to fix that. "I'll let you off easy and bait your hook for you."

He'd expected gratitude—women by and large never seemed too eager to spear a worm and sink it underwater to its doom—but she surprised him.

"What?" Karla woke right up, dark eyebrows arching in defiance. "Don't think I can handle it?" She snatched the fishing rod from his hands. "I can bait my own hook, thank you very much."

"Hey—" Dylan held his hands up "—no problem. Just wanted to be sure you were awake enough to handle sharp objects." He found the plastic tub of night crawlers he'd brought and handed it to her before tending to his own rod.

This woman had an independent streak a mile wide. He got that. But what was the story behind her strong aversion to accepting help? When he allowed himself a moment to think about it, what really bugged him was that she seemed easily able to tap into the assistance someone like Jim Shoemacher offered, but she bristled at the simple courtesy of a baited hook from him. He knew his history was skewing that response. The last woman he'd taken out on this boat had been Yvonne, and she'd spent the day hinting she'd have rather been on something larger, more upscale like the *High Tide*. In a backhanded way, Yvonne had planted the seed for his charter company, but he still had no interest in showing any gratitude for that. Some wounds left marks for a long time.

As it turned out, Karla did a deplorable job of baiting a hook, spearing the worm so delicately it disappeared from the line at the first nibble. He wasn't about to point that out, though—at least not until she asked.

They spent the first fifteen minutes of actual fishing in companionable silence. Dylan found that refreshing. He'd tried not to compare it to Yvonne's exasperating compulsion to fill the silence with chatter, but the differences between the two women kept assailing him. Upscale, blonde Yvonne was about as different from Karla—emotionally, spiritually, even physically—as a woman could get. Under other circumstances, that might make Karla very attractive to him. Knowing she was heading back to Chicago and why, however, did a good job of squelching that notion.

He watched her peer down into the water with that analytical, problem-solving glare of hers, reel her line in, and then turn to stare at him. "I'm not doing this right."

"Well, you've got the basic concept. You just need a little technique."

She held out the rod to him. "Show me." *Well, what do you know? A request for help.*

He complied. She yawned and slid over next

to him, watching as he showed her what to do. Just as he handed the rod back to her, his own rod bent with a "hit," followed by the exhilarating whirr of the line being pulled out by a sizable fish.

"You got one!" Karla's eyes popped wide-awake.

"Well, not yet." He grabbed the line and began to pull up slightly. "Now comes the fun part."

Two minutes later, it was hard to say who was more pleased at the nice big fish that landed on the boat floor—he or Karla. The fun had begun, sparking that glow in Dylan's chest of which he never hoped to tire: landing a big fish. She pointed at the rainbow of scales, asked questions about the species—and how good it was to eat—all sorts of things. It was a pleasure to watch her curiosity get the better of her. Dylan found himself looking forward to what she'd be like when she caught her own fish.

Just as the sun rose fully above the top of the trees, Karla's line bobbed and whirred, making her jump and yelp with something just short of glee. He laughed, expecting some excitement but not her over-the-top joy. "Okay now," he coached, surprised by how invested he'd become in her success, "pull up slowly, then reel the line in as you bring the rod back down." She followed his instructions, her rod bending in so deep an arc that Dylan entertained the thought she might land a whopper. Wouldn't that be fun to watch her waltz into town with the season's largest trophy to date?

"There's a monster on the other end of this line," she said, perhaps reading his expression of surprise.

"Beginner's luck, maybe."

"Jonah and the whale, more likely."

Dylan thought that an odd comment, but didn't pursue it in the face of the present excitement. "Keep going, let him tire himself out so he doesn't snap the line. That's right. He's definitely a good-size fish."

Karla raised and lowered the line as instructed, reeling the fish closer in. Then some thought struck her—it showed all over her face—and she turned to him. "Hey, how do you know it's a *he*? Don't lady fish put up a good fight?"

They certainly do, Dylan thought. "Okay, reel *him or her* in slowly," he corrected, not hiding the amusement in his voice. It was always gratifying to watch a customer land a good catch, but this was enjoyable on a whole other level. The first was work success, while this was just plain fun. Where had all his joy gone lately? Worse yet, until this moment, he hadn't even missed it.

Dylan stowed his own line to concentrate on helping her—this one was not going to get away if he could help it. As she kept reeling the line in, Dylan came up behind her and placed a finger on her line to test the tension. She smelled like coffee and a subtle sort of spice. His mind seemed eager to gather small details like that, adding to the complex picture of her forming in his mind. He'd painted all women with the same suspicious brush ever since Yvonne—his reaction to Karla unsettled as much as it surprised him.

"I'm losing him!" she squeaked when the line bent deeply toward the water.

"No, no you're not—he's just closer." Dylan pointed to the large shadow curling through the water just off to her left. "Look." It was, indeed, a very big fish.

"Oh." Wonder and anticipation and competitiveness all in one syllable.

Dylan's pulse quickened as he leaned over her shoulder to help her hold the rod. "Just a bit more, let him go for a bit and pull up slowly."

"Look at the size of him," she marveled as the fish arced up toward the surface, a rainbow of silvery fins and bubbles.

Well, what do you know? "Biggest one this year, maybe."

She turned to look at him. "No."

"No kidding. You're about to gain some serious Gordon Falls street credibility when you land this."

She laughed, then caught her breath as the fish broke the water to flap furiously. "Help!"

He grabbed the net from behind the seats, genuinely thrilled for her. "Steady, you're doing fine. Bring him close to the boat if you can."

Seconds later Dylan scooped up what surely was the largest catch of his season so far—a trophy-worthy nine-pound walleye that pounded against the boat floor and sent droplets flying over the both of them.

The only thing larger than the fish was the size of Karla's grin. That, and the defiant cord of affection that was untangling inside Dylan despite his every effort to stop it.

It was just a fish. Granted, it was a big fish, and Dylan seemed about to burst with pride that she'd landed it, but it wasn't as if she'd never caught a fish before. She'd just never felt this way about catching one before. It was hokey, really, the giddy way she held up the thing for Dylan's photograph. As if some switch had turned her back into her five-year-old self, back before she could catch on to the tension between her father and grandfather, back when the world was perfect and full of wonder. Maybe the world was turning back to perfect and full of wonder—the past twelve hours sure had been filled with both.

Karla pulled the string on the bakery box of cheese Danish—after a hefty dose of hand sanitizer, of course—and unscrewed the lid on the thermos of cinnamon-hazelnut coffee she'd brought. This wasn't the most elegant breakfast she'd ever served, but it was fast turning into one of the most pleasant. The sun had come up fully, bathing the boat in warmth and scattering sparkles on the river around them. Birdsong poked through the peaceful quiet, and the gentle rocking of the boat soothed out tensions Karla hadn't even realized she was holding.

She stared at the enormous fish—*her* enormous fish—now iced in a cooler at the end of the boat.

"Wow," Dylan sighed behind a mouthful of Danish. "You are so good at what you do."

Karla nodded at him. "Evidently, so are you."

"I think we'll make a pretty good team." He said it carefully, tentatively, as if broaching the subject of their pairing was dangerous territory. "For the anniversary thing, I mean."

"It's worth celebrating," she offered, hoisting the coffee in a toast. "Firemen are important." After pouring herself what must be her sixth cup of the morning, she asked. "Did you always want to be a fireman?"

"Well, I think all little boys want to be firemen. Or astronauts or whatever. I came on the department because of my uncle."

"Is he a fireman?"

"No, actually, he's a missionary in Nigeria. But after my—" he chose his next words carefully "—exodus from Chicago…we had a few long phone conversations while he was home on furlough. I needed ways to make my life about more than it had been."

He'd brought it up, so Karla decided it was safe to ask. He'd only mentioned what he did in the most basic of terms when they'd spoken of his time in Chicago before. "Which had been what?"

Dylan sat back and put one foot up on the side of the boat. "You know those guys from the first catch? The power dudes all shouting their accomplishments at each other over breakfast?"

She wouldn't categorize the men quite that severely, but she knew the stereotype. She'd studied them, in fact; they would be the ideal customer for her place once it opened. They were Perk's target clientele, which was what made the Clifton internship such a prize. "Jim Shoe?"

"You might say I was on the Jim Shoe track. Suit, tie, car I could only barely afford, all the trimmings. My own little cubicle in one of those great big glass boxes."

He'd mentioned that before, but Karla still couldn't transplant the rugged outdoorsman in front of her into such a slick setting. If he'd been "upwardly mobile," he'd left it far behind since then. "Jim Shoe's a nice guy."

"Some of them are. I'm not saying it's a bad way to be, but only if you want it." A muscle in his jaw tightened with the last two words. He'd either stopped wanting it, or never wanted it in the first place. Before she could ask, he answered for her. "I didn't. Well, not really. I only thought I did. Or someone had me thinking I did."

"Who?" Karla was amazed she had the nerve to ask; it was clear the subject was touchy for him.

Dylan shifted and stared into his coffee. "Her name was Yvonne. We met through a friend of hers. She had more drive than anyone I'd ever met. A real powerhouse, you know? When Yvonne walked into a room, everyone knew. I felt like the luckiest guy in the world to have her pick me out." He braved a glance at Karla, and she felt her whole body react to the pain in his eyes. "Only I didn't end up so lucky. I loved her, and I think, in her way, she loved me. She had all these plans— big, amazing plans that made me feel like the two of us would be unstoppable. One of those power couples you read about."

Karla waited a long time before she asked, "What happened?"

Dylan picked up a fishing lure and began twirling it between two fingers. "The plans were fabulous at first. I felt like the world was my oyster. Then the decisions got harder. The price got higher. Things started to sit wrong on me. I'd start to talk about a doubt, or a worry, and Yvonne would always talk me out of it, write it off as the price of a dynamite career or whatever." He exhaled roughly. "After a while the price began including stepping on other people, grabbing credit or connections or hobnobbing with people I didn't even like. The whole thing just sort of lost its shine."

He tossed the lure back in the tackle box. "One day I looked at my closetful of nice suits and realized I didn't want to put any of them on. They felt like lead on my shoulders."

"So you left?"

"No, not right away. But my boss would tell you I lost 'the fire in my belly.' One of his favorite sayings, which I never liked much anyway. And then, just when I was thinking about proposing—I suppose I thought I needed something drastic to shake me out of my funk—Yvonne informed me she'd taken up with my boss and that she hoped that wouldn't be too awkward at the office."

He whacked the tackle box shut and flipped the latch with a sharp snap. "Evidently the office party where I had the flu opened up a whole new opportunity for Yvonne. And to think I told her to stay and have a good time while I got a cab home."

What was there to say to a story like that? "Wow. I'm sorry."

Dylan hadn't moved his eyes up from the tackle box. "Yeah, well, better to find out before things got any more serious. I suppose someday I'll thank her for that."

Karla felt the sharp edges of his bitter words. No wonder Dylan struck her as immensely loyal—he'd been betrayed in the worst possible way by a woman who had clearly meant the world to him. Her love life—if one could call the string of lukewarm relationships she'd had a "love life"—didn't carry anything close to that kind of pain. "How did you manage to get through something like that?"

That question brought his eyes up to her. "Not well, if you're looking for advice. I just sort of stopped. I mean, I was a walking, breathing person, but not much more. I went through the motions of work, I ate food, I sat in a church pew on Sundays—which is a different thing than going to church, by the way. It was summer so I spent a lot of time just sitting on the lakefront looking at the water, wishing I was somewhere else."

Funny, she'd spent the first few mornings of her stay in Gordon Falls looking at the river wishing *she* was somewhere else. "How did you end up here?"

"George Bradens is a friend of my father's. I'd been here once or twice on a weekend vacation, that sort of thing—nothing like the time you'd spent here, but I'd always liked it." He hesitated for a moment. "My dad is big into fishing, but I'd never had time once I got out of school, you know? Always too busy climbing the next rung of the ladder. Well, one day I walked by a news store and for some reason picked up a boating magazine." Dylan ran his hand along the railing of the boat. "And a little puff of something blew back into me. As if the whole dark wall of 'not here' finally had broken open into 'somewhere else,' if that makes any sense."

Karla brought her knees up to her chin and hugged them. "It makes a lot of sense. Knowing where you need to go is half the battle, sometimes." She thought about the zing of energy that had hit her when she'd replied to Chef Daniel, a zing that hadn't left her yet, tired as she was.

He leaned back, soaking in the now-full morning sunshine. "Says the woman with a clear plan in her head. You know exactly where you want to go, don't you?"

She considered telling him about the Clifton internship—she certainly was dying to celebrate it with somebody—but it seemed unfair, given the story he was telling. "I have lots of plans, yes."

"Don't let my sour state kill any of that for you. Jim Shoe is right—you're going places."

He held her eyes for just a moment, something sad and slightly angry casting a shadow over his gaze. As if he decided "going places" was a country he could no longer go nor cared to visit. Karla's heart pinched in an unsettling urge to see a man like Dylan treated in the way he deserved rather than the way Yvonne had discarded him. Just for a second, something hummed in the air between them.

And then it was gone. Dylan stood up, effectively changing the subject. "So, are you going to mount your amazing fish, or eat it?" He turned from her to step onto the bow to pull up anchor.

Karla entertained a comical vision of the huge fish mounted gaping-mouthed on the wall behind the cash register in her future coffee shop. Or funnier still, gracing the elegant walls of Perk. What on earth would she ever do with a trophy fish? "Oh, eat it, definitely."

"Good call. I'd say let me know if you need a recipe, but you probably have four."

She didn't have a single one. Grandpa, however, probably had twelve.

Chapter Seven

"Three mocha lattes, two cinnamon cappuccinos, and one chai tea." Karla walked around the six middle-aged women on Tuesday morning, enjoying the smiles of gratitude as she set down the appropriate coffees in front of each one. If the earlier group of businessmen had been satisfied, this group of nuns from Iowa were in absolute bliss. Dylan had obviously given them a fabulous trip this morning, the way they gushed and boasted over their fine catches. "Oh, and the dozen cranberry-orange scones you ordered are coming right up."

More glee. Karla would have thought she was handing out chocolate to children for all the delightful anticipation she saw around the table. Funny how a simple idea like the Coffee Catch had such a positive effect on Dylan's customers. It made her feel good about her own future prospects when she started at Perk, and when she opened a place of her own.

"You know," said a round-faced nun with cheery eyes, "I've been to Gordon Falls dozens of times and never stopped in here. Look what I was missing!"

"We heard your grandfather was laid up with a hip operation," said another of the sisters. "I told Captain McDonald we'd pray for his speedy recovery, but it looks like you've got things well in hand, young lady." Her eye took on an extra sparkle. "And we heard about your fish!"

Karla looked up to catch Dylan's eye as he walked in the door. She made a point of specially greeting the Catch customers as he was always about ten minutes behind them settling things on the dock.

"Captain McDonald is a great guide, and I ate the fillets to prove it. So he helped you find all the best fish this morning?" Karla emphasized the *Captain* loud enough for Dylan to hear, raising a teasing eyebrow as she headed back to the counter for the plate of scones.

A chorus of approval from the table turned Dylan's cheeks red and made Karla laugh. "Seems this morning was a big hit."

"Honestly, it's been like taking my grandmother fishing. Times six," Dylan whispered, veering to intercept Karla in her path to the counter. "One of them actually pinched my cheek."

"Sounds like they've had a wonderful morning," she replied, finding his befuddlement more than a bit amusing. Then, because she couldn't help herself, she managed a small salute and a "Sir."

"Look!" Emily's excited cry pulled Karla away from any further ribbing. The waitress held up a cup and saucer overflowing down one side with creamy milk froth. "I did it!"

"You sure did." Karla had to admire Emily's persistence in learning to work the espresso machine. She didn't have the heart to tell the waitress that the machine would be returning to Chicago with her when she left in a month. Then again, maybe not. The success of the Coffee Catch might convince Grandpa to invest in one anyway. She'd told her parents about the wonderful apprenticeship at the Clifton, but hadn't been able to tell her grandfather. No matter how many times she reminded him she was just here to help out, he seemed all too ready to install her behind the counter permanently.

"I'm not sure how it will taste," Emily said, "but at least this one looks right and stayed in the cup. Mostly." She handed Karla the cup and saucer with eager eyes. "You be the judge."

The brew could have tasted ten times worse than it did and Karla would still have pasted an appreciative look on her face. "It's pretty close," she exaggerated, ignoring the sharp taste and too-cool temperature of the drink. Emily was trying so hard, and the machine had seemed so foreign to the sturdy old wait-ress. "You'll be putting me out of a job in no time."

"Oh, I'd never want that. Karl's thrilled to pieces you're behind the counter. Told me so himself the other day when I visited him be-fore my shift." Her eyes took on a beam to match the sisters' glowing expressions. "He's so proud of you. And now with the big event you've taken on…well, I thought he'd just about bust his buttons over you. And The Fish!"

"That was pretty amazing." Everyone had simply started calling it "The Fish." The thing was edging toward legend. It made her almost regret eating it rather than mounting it, but what would she do with a trophy like that?

Fast as the news of her big catch had spread, Karla wasn't at all surprised that word had also swept through town over the weekend about the anniversary committee chairmanship. She sighed as she arranged scones on a little footed cake stand. Karl's Koffee was the epicenter of Gordon Falls gossip because Karl Kennedy knew everybody's business. When someone was sick or hurt or grieving, that skill often made sure help was on the way. On the other hand, nothing ever said within earshot of Karl's Koffee stayed private for very long.

"I think you and Dylan will do a bang-up job on the party," Emily went on. "I've already talked the gals down at the library into doing a boat...er, float, or whatever you'll call it."

Karla put the last of the scones in its place and picked up a stack of small plates. "That's great, Emily. I'll make sure you know when the sign-up sheet is ready."

"Silliest thing I ever heard of," grumbled Oscar Halverson, owner of the local grocery store. The old man could always be counted on to find the dark cloud in any situation. Grandpa called him Oscar the Grouch after the Sesame Street character—sometimes even to his face.

"Careful, Oscar," Dylan chided. "Keep up that kind of endorsement and you'll end up in charge of decorations. By the way," he went on, parking himself on the counter seat next to Halverson and leaning in, "you might want to stock up on those tiny strings of Christmas lights. Folks will be wanting them and if you're the only place carrying a good selection in the middle of July, you could clean up."

That cleared most of the scowl off Oscar's face. "You're probably telling that to half a dozen businesses in town."

"Just you so far." Dylan pointed at him. "You remember that when it comes time to buy advertising in the banquet program."

Oscar grumbled into his coffee mug and slid his two quarters onto the counter. Grandpa had been charging Oscar fifty cents for a single cup of coffee since Karla was in the first grade. The old man would probably stop coming if Karl ever raised it to the dollar he charged everyone else. How Grandpa managed to keep track of the special attention and various considerations he'd extended to hundreds of customers over the years, Karla could never fathom. His hip may have failed, but his mind was as sharp as ever.

"Oh, Captain McDonald, we've had such fun this morning. I love our yearly retreats but already this one has been the best by far." One of the sisters, whom Karla had heard boasting of the day's largest catch, beamed at Dylan.

"And we've only just started," added another. "Our Lord and his disciples were fishermen, too. It's a perfect match—I don't know why we hadn't thought of it before."

"What's the rest of your retreat look like?" Dylan pulled a chair up beside the sisters' table and sat on it backward. The posture gave him a rakish, playful quality, and the women ate it up faster than the scones.

"Three days of peace, rest, prayer and fellowship in a set of cabins overlooking the river out by the state park. The coffee won't be as fine, but the view takes your breath away."

Dylan smiled. "I know that place. Beautiful."

The sister nearest Dylan put a hand on his broad shoulder. "We do lots of our best praying at our retreats. What can we pray for you, Captain? You've given us such a fine time— we'd like to repay the favor."

Karla stilled. She'd seen him Sundays at church, knew him to be a man of faith, but wanted to see how Dylan would respond to such a request.

His smile was warm and genuine. "As if I didn't find you all sweet enough already." He gave the sister's question a moment's consideration. "Well, I'll tell you. Karla here and I have been roped into a pretty big job over the next few weeks." He lifted his gaze to Karla and she felt her throat tighten. "We're going to need a lot of wisdom on how to pull it off the right way. And it's going to take lots of folks coming on board and being nice to each other. That's not always the easiest thing to manage in a small town, you know. So, I guess I'd appreciate prayers for the firehouse's 150th anniversary celebration, and for Karla and I while we pull it together."

The smiles and "aww"s from around the table were endearing. These fishing nuns were just about the kindest women Karla had ever met. It struck her that she'd probably never see an exchange like that at Perk. And that was okay—Chicago was Chicago, and a small town had a totally different atmosphere.

"We'd be honored to pray for both of you and the firehouse, as well. It's a fine thing you volunteer firemen do. Oh—fire*fighters*," the sister corrected herself, "you told me you have a lady fireman in your department, don't you?"

Karla had met JJ Cushman, the department's first female volunteer firefighter. She was a pretty impressive woman. Her husband, Alex, was a smart businessman, too, and she'd planned to make sure she sat down and got Alex's business advice before leaving Gordon

Falls. Maybe she and Dylan could make sure Alex had a role on the anniversary committee.

She and Dylan. Karla still wasn't quite sure how that pairing sat with her. He was a truly amazing guy, but Gordon Falls had always been just a layover on her career flight path. She wasn't blind, however, to how quickly and enthusiastically the town seemed to be nudging them together.

"Thank you very much for your prayers, sisters." Dylan smiled at each of the six women. "I'm sure we're going to need them."

"Yes," Karla added, feeling a bit odd but also incredibly thankful. "It's appreciated."

"Oh! We're running behind." The youngest of the sisters checked her watch. "Finish up your coffees, gals. We're due at the cabins in twenty minutes."

"Thank goodness for Eliza," another sister said. "She keeps us on schedule."

Within minutes, Karla had the remaining scones packed up—with a few extras on the house—and even got a hug from one or two of the nuns as they piled out of the coffee shop and into their minivan.

"Coffee Catch Number Two," Dylan sighed as he waved from the shop's large front windows. "Even more successful than the first. Karla, I think we're absolutely onto something."

* * *

Dylan sat at the small table belowdecks in the *High Tide* that afternoon and punched the calculator numbers again. He preferred to do paperwork in the tiny cabin of the boat than on the large desk at his apartment. The surroundings of the *High Tide* made it easy to remember why all this struggle was worth it.

It was working, if only barely. *Thank You, Lord, that things are picking up.* Thing were going okay before, but just enough to cover the loan payments. His stockpile of savings was nearing its end, and Dylan wanted Gordon River Fishing Charters to start pulling ahead of expenses by the end of the summer. This was a seasonal business, after all, so he needed strong tourist seasons to carry him through when summer was over.

The end of summer—the end of Karla's stay in Gordon Falls. Part of Dylan didn't want to see her go. That was dumb, because she was always planning on going back to Chicago; nothing had changed.

He tapped his cell phone on and pulled up the photo of Karla holding the enormous fish. When he'd shown it to his sister, she'd suggested it become the cover of his business brochure. It wasn't a bad idea; every fisherman dreamed of landing such a prize. Dylan just wasn't sure he was ready to stare at Karla's beaming face on a daily basis. He was doing that now, and it was unraveling things in his chest he'd preferred to stay tightly knotted.

I'm grateful for her help, Lord, he shared with God as he fingered the image. *You know I am. But what's going on here? Why do I feel this connection when You know nothing can come of it?*

He'd written women off entirely after Yvonne. A drastic attitude—he knew that—but it was self-preservation. Even now, just the memory of the dismissal in her eyes when she told him she'd taken up with his boss could blow a dark hole in his stomach. He'd been *so wrong* about her. *I don't ever want to feel that way again. I'd rather be alone.*

But was the choice really that severe? God's plan for him had to be larger than the two options of hurt or alone. Karla was helpful and friendly. Maybe a helpful friend was the best way to restore his faith in the female gender. One look around town gave him hard evidence that not all women were predatory— there had been a wave of happy marriages in the fire department lately, right in front of his nose. He wasn't ready for a relationship. But striking up a friendship with someone who was leaving in a month? Well, that seemed as good a way as any to stick his toe back in the water.

After all, they'd be spending enough time together pulling off the Fire Department Anniversary Boat Parade. Might as well enjoy it.

Chapter Eight

Violet clasped her hands together as Karla held up the square of dense cotton yarn now knit and draping from her needles. "Look at you!" Violet said. "You're a natural, I tell you. My first dishcloths were loads worse."

Karla's visits to the Gordon Falls Community Church Knitting Circle were a much-needed break. In many ways this group was as nurturing and vivacious as the nuns she had served yesterday morning. "It was easy once I remembered." Her mother had taught her as a girl, but the yarn and needles had given way to flour and cookie cutters as soon as Karla was old enough to work the oven on her own. "This pot holder pattern is super easy anyway. I'm not so sure I could stick with it long enough to do those big prayer shawls like you do."

The group met once a week to knit soft, fluffy wraps that were prayed over and given to anyone in the community who needed healing or comfort. Grandpa had one especially made for him by Violet, who was currently waving Karla's comment away. "A square, a rectangle, same difference. You may knit a bit tight for a prayer shawl, but it's perfect for pot holders and place mats." Violet winked. "Just dense enough, eh?"

Karla found herself laughing. It was a common occurrence in Violet Sharpton's company. "You say that like it's a compliment."

"It is, sweetheart. Besides, prayer shawls are more a work of the heart than of the needles. Takes a lot of patience and caring, and you're using up all you got of those right now on your grandfather." She leaned in. "To tell you the truth, we both are. Your grandpa can be an old goat when he wants to be."

Karla snipped off the thick cotton yarn—a sunny yellow in this case—and began to work it through the final knot. While Grandpa was at his checkups, she'd made a half dozen new pot holders for the shop, all in cheery ice-cream colors. "Tell me about it."

Violet's gaze softened. "He had another argument with your father last night, didn't he?"

Sighing, Karla put the finished pot holder in

her bag alongside its rainbow of companions. The vibrant colors had been Violet's idea, a way to brighten up the long hours of waiting and coping. For the most part, it had worked—Karla was surprised that knitting could give her almost the same solace as baking and brewing, and the work was much more portable. "Dad's stressed out over the shuffle back and forth to his office. It's been…"

Violet held up her hands. "'Nuff said. Fathers and sons, sons and fathers. Come to think of it, I think they can *both* be old goats some days. How's your mama holding up?"

Karla cast on the two dozen stitches to start another pot holder—this one a bright lime green. Talking to Violet was like breathing clean air away from the tension of Grandpa's house or the emptiness of her place above the coffee shop. As such, she wasn't in any hurry to leave the church meeting room where everyone was knitting. They were all making prayer shawls, but Vi had organized a "special pass" for Karla to come and "decompress over the needles" anytime she felt she needed company. She'd shown up every week since.

Today she ought to have her nose in a textbook or online notes, but this morning had been a rough one at the coffee shop and she wasn't eager to head on over to Grandpa's.

"Mom can slough it off a bit better than Dad can, so she's holding up okay. Only I'm pretty sure she's ready to go back home tomorrow now that Grandpa can manage with just Dad."

"Two weeks more, isn't that what doctor said?" an older woman named Tina asked.

"If he behaves himself," Karla answered.

"Which isn't likely," Violet added.

"I heard all about The Fish," Melba Bradens added, and Karla sent her a smile of thanks for changing the subject. "You've shown up all the guys by catching such a whopper. The women of Gordon Falls owe you a debt of gratitude."

"It made a fabulous meal," Karla replied, still unable to stop smiling when she recalled Grandpa's eyes as he peered into the cooler at the enormous fish when Dylan had deposited it in the house kitchen. He hadn't stopped talking about it yet.

"I still think you could have had it mounted and displayed at Karl's." Melba winked. "A permanent reminder that fisher*women* exist. You and JJ serve as good reminders in this town."

Karla hadn't thought of herself as having a kinship with the fire department's first and so far only female firefighter, but at the idea of their connection a warm spot bloomed under her ribs. "None of my Chicago friends can believe it, even though I sent everyone a photo."

"Dylan put one up on the firehouse bulletin board," said Jeannie Owens, who Karla remembered was married to the fire inspector. "He told Clark he's thinking about using it as the cover for his business brochures. It's certainly a ringing endorsement for his charter business."

"It's certainly a ringing endorsement for Dylan," Abby Reed mused, weighting her words with a few assumptions Karla would just as soon do without.

She was trying to convince herself the warm thoughts she held for that morning were mostly about the trophy fish, but it wasn't working. Her mind kept recalling the way the slanted morning sunshine brought out colors in his cobalt-blue eyes. Karla also remembered the shadows of pain that lingered there as he talked about what that woman Yvonne had done to him. She'd broken his heart. The knowledge of that wound deepened how she saw the man, accentuated her awareness of his character and loyalty. Karla sighed. She spent too much time thinking about him. Unfortunately, that wasn't about to change anytime soon. Dylan was due in tomorrow morning with the third Coffee Catch, and then they had to get ready for another anniversary committee meeting. From a purely logical standpoint, Karla regretted how he was growing on her.

She was leaving. The internship at Perk began a little over three weeks from now, and she'd still not been able to tell anyone but Mom and Dad, whom she'd sworn to secrecy. She couldn't speak of it to Dylan, or the friendly ladies who were her present company, because it would be too easy for word to get back to Grandpa. She knew her departure would hurt him, and he was already so down over his slow progress healing.

"Well, I'll tell you, not everyone is thrilled about your big fish," Marge countered. "Oscar Halverson was going on and on at the market yesterday how the 'tourists were getting all the good fish.'" She leaned in toward Karla. "I think he's jealous. He's probably told stories about that big one eluding him all these years." She smiled victoriously at Karla as she turned her work and began knitting a new row. "But I couldn't be happier for you. Cocaptain of the boat parade and now this. It's the biggest splash of an entry into Gordon Falls in years."

"Oh, Marge, you always did have a way with words." Tina hid behind a hand as she chuckled. "But you're right—Oscar's green with envy. Probably best you didn't mount the fish, Karla. Karl would probably insist it hang in his shop, and then Oscar would only stare at it every day with his discount coffee and grumble." She imitated Oscar's thick mustache with her fingers and mimicked his frown so accurately that she got a laugh from the whole group. Even Karla could clearly picture the old man glaring at a glassy-eyed fish from behind his coffee mug. Grandpa surely would never miss an opportunity to rub it in that his flesh and blood had landed The Fish. He was already boasting to everyone who would listen.

"Maybe we should make Oscar a prayer shawl," Melba said, holding in a chuckle. "Violet could put a great big fish on it."

"Someone ought to do something to soften Oscar's rough edges," Jeannie said, "but I don't think that's an appropriate use of a prayer shawl." When everyone reluctantly agreed, she added softly, "But it is funny to think about."

"Grandpa loves his," Karla told Violet for what had to be the tenth time. She wasn't too young to see the sparks flying between these two seniors. Mom and Dad refused to talk about it, but Karla couldn't help thinking Violet might be just what Grandpa Karl needed to kick him back into life.

"I prayed so much patience into that thing," Violet said, closing her eyes as if to mimic the process, "but I'm not seeing much of a result. He's as antsy as ever, if you ask me."

"You should have seen him last night, Vi," Karla replied. "He fell asleep with it draped around his shoulders. He kept fingering the fringe." *As if he was holding your hand,* Karla added silently. She couldn't be the only person to catch on to what was blooming between Grandpa and Violet, could she?

The more important question might be: Was anyone catching on to what was simmering between her and Dylan? These women were shameless matchmakers, and the last thing they needed was any encouragement in that department.

The Coffee Catches just kept getting better and better. Today's six pharmaceutical salesmen in from Iowa City had such a banner morning, Dylan was sure the Gordon River was running out of fish. By the time he'd cleaned and packaged their haul, they were just on their way out the door. The hearty handshakes and promises of return visits were welcome, but Dylan found himself exhausted as he slid into a counter seat at Karl's. From the sag in her shoulder and the frizz in her hair, Karla's morning had been just as demanding.

"Busy morning?" he asked, looking after the trio of dark sedans as they pulled out of the parking places.

Karla blew one of her dark wispy bangs out of her eyes. "They ordered enormous breakfasts, every one of them. Said it was 'nonstop reeling 'em in' from the moment you dropped anchor. Evidently good fishing makes you hungry."

"I'm starved," Dylan admitted. "Got any eggs left back there?"

"Usually I have a chance to grab some breakfast, but I haven't even eaten yet myself." Karla looked across the room while she emptied her apron pockets into the cash register. "The corner booth is open. Let's you and I grab it and we can both eat while we plan for tomorrow night." She left a basic breakfast order with Emily and then headed toward the booth.

The corner booth at Karl's. She did realize there wasn't a more public place for two people to be eating in all of Gordon Falls, didn't she? Part of him wanted to warn her off the idea—tongues would be wagging within the hour, especially since he'd run into Abby Reed, one of the town's more "talkative" residents, on his way in. He was supposed to be fending off the town's urge to pair him with Karla; sharing the corner booth with her would only send Abby into matchmaking mode.

Then again, Dylan couldn't think of anything he'd rather do more than sit down and eat a huge, relaxing breakfast with Karla. Groups of friends used the corner booth all the time. It was just a table in a coffee shop, for crying out loud. It wasn't as if everyone was watching.

Of course it was as if everyone was watching. Abby Reed practically gave herself a sprained shoulder trying to peer around the corner as he and Karla slid into the booth beneath Karl's big river-view front window.

"I thought you'd like to know I got a call from Jim Shoemacher yesterday." Dylan made sure he spoke about business loud enough for Abby to hear. "He booked two more fishing trips for him and his friends. And he asked if I had brochures or a website. I told him about your fish, and that I'd like to use your photo on the brochures. He thought it was a great idea"

"You've got a website up and running, don't you?" Knowing Karla, she had plans all drawn up for hers. He'd seen what she called her "dream file"—it was thick and labeled and even color coded—in that great big bag she lugged around.

"Not really. I've been meaning to, but so far I've only bought a listing in a couple of tourism books and took an ad out in a few local sporting magazines."

Karla looked as though he'd broken twelve laws. "Well, no wonder you're still looking for business. That stuff's essential these days." Her eyes narrowed as Emily set down silverware and two coffee mugs. "Wow, you really hate marketing, don't you?"

"I didn't come to Gordon Falls to check my email. So we're having good old-fashioned coffee this morning?"

"I'm too wiped to make anything fancier than ice water," Karla said, tucking her hair behind her ears. Her dark hair had this intriguing way of curling against her cheek when she didn't push it behind her ears. It made him want to reach out and free the locks back up again, which was a stupid impulse if ever there was one.

Emily returned and filled the cups. Dylan was fine with that; Karl had always made good coffee. Karla, however, looked as if she were "making do." It made him laugh a bit as he spooned sugar into his cup. "You're more tired than you were the day of The Fish."

"I was up late turning in a project for one of my online courses." She yawned. "Cash flow projection and inventory analysis. Thrilling stuff, I tell you. I want to bake and brew, not add and subtract."

He mimicked her earlier comment. "Wow, you really hate administration, don't you?"

"Point taken." She took a sip of coffee. "Hey, Jim Shoemacher must have Gordon Falls on the brain. He sent me an email yesterday to ask how things were going with the shop. I told him about another thing I'm working on, something to do with a Chicago place I thought he might know. He made an offer again to help me find a location when I was ready."

"You should take him up on it. I get the feeling that's one influential gym shoe." Dylan knew a power player when he saw one. His boss had been one—right up until he had helped himself to Dylan's future fiancée. Or Yvonne had helped herself to his boss— frankly, he couldn't say which and he didn't care. Much.

"I could use a guy like him in my corner," she admitted. "I know how many eateries fold in their first year. They made us study the statistics. If I didn't believe in a Sovereign God, I might be tempted to just toss in the scones after last night's textbook chapter. Depressing."

Dylan had always felt God calling him to Gordon Falls; he'd just gotten very good at "mishearing" the message. "So you're sure the bakeshop—or breakfast place, or whatever you're going to call it—is where God wants you to be, huh?"

"Absolutely." That indescribable kindle of energy returned to her eyes at the mere mention of the shop. The same spark that had drawn him in when she made the first latte for him.

He told himself it was fun to watch a friend on the brink of what they were born to do. Maybe it would energize him in the process. "What are you going to call it? The new place, I mean?"

"Rooster's."

That wasn't what he was expecting. "Rooster's?"

"You know, like the bird that crows. Roosters are leaders—they're the ones launching the day, calling everyone else to get up and get going." The fatigue melted off her body as she spoke with animation and began waving her hands about. "They're colorful and a bit cocky and absolutely necessary to a farm's success. I think God had fun when He made roosters. My customers are going to be the world's roosters, and I'm going to help them launch their day." She had every detail of her place vividly fixed in her imagination; he could see it all over her face.

"I suppose I don't need to ask if you have a logo?" She smiled, and Dylan knew somewhere in that massively organized notebook of hers she probably had four. "Will you show me someday?"

"Maybe."

Emily arrived with two heaping plates of simple scrambled eggs and toast. Dylan was grateful for the hot breakfast and the strong coffee. "Simple pleasures." He looked up at her. "Or don't you think so?"

"No, I like a good egg as much as the next person. But nothing I serve will be ordinary. Everything's going to have a unique flair, something creative."

"Want me to say grace?"

"Sure."

Normally, Dylan was in the habit of taking hands across a table for grace, but that wasn't a smart idea in this case. Not only would it give the gossips of Karl's Koffee loads to talk about, but Dylan knew from his time on the boat with her that there was nothing ordinary in touching Karla. That energy of hers zinged into him whenever they had contact. Holding hands felt like a giant leap into a place he absolutely shouldn't go.

He said a quick, awkward and rather distracted grace, grateful for the smile she gave him when they dug into their eggs. He didn't know much about himself lately, but he was pretty certain he wasn't a rooster. Not anymore.

Chapter Nine

The guys sat around the firehouse table a few days later, tossing back root beers and throwing around ideas to decorate Dylan's boat for the parade down the river. "I can't stop using the boat, so the decorations will have to be something we can make here and then attach the night before." Fond as he was of the parade idea, he wasn't in a position to sacrifice any potential charters just so that his boat could play dress-up.

"You said we're leading the parade, right? It's gonna have to be really good." Jesse Sykes looked around the table. "Guys, this is way out of our league."

"Charlotte's got that kind of skill," suggested Yorky, one of the older members of the department and one with a particularly soft spot for Jesse's girlfriend. "And she works in the store with all that crafty stuff. Won't she help us out?"

"I'm sure she will," Jessie replied, "and I can take care of a lot of the structural part." When he wasn't at the firehouse, Jesse had a home construction and renovation business. "But we still need a decent idea."

"What color is a 150th wedding anniversary? You know, like silver, gold, that sort of thing?" Wally asked.

Chad Owens, the fire inspector who just happened to be in the room, laughed from behind Dylan. "Your average married couple does not get to a 150th anniversary, Wally. You'd have to live to be 170."

"Oh, yeah, right. Well, you oughta know." Chad was younger than Yorky, for that matter, but his seriousness earned him a bit of an "old man" reputation around the firehouse. It made Dylan wonder how he'd ever won the heart of someone so youthful and energetic as his wife, Jeannie, who ran the town's confectionary. Talk about a case of opposites attracting…

"What if we turned it into a log cabin like the old resort that used to be in town." Jesse leaned in. "You know, the one Chief Bradens's father-in-law ran?"

"Oh, and what if we could rig it so that

paper flames came out the window," Wally added, getting excited. "And then we could pump water from the river and spray everyone as we pretended to put out the fire."

"That'd be dramatic," Yorky said with a bit of skepticism. "And complicated."

"Not really," countered Jesse, who had a flair for both the dramatic and the complicated. Dylan swallowed hard at the thought of his beloved boat being encased in fake logs and engulfed in paper flames. Then again, if the floats were a competition, how could something like that lose? "Actually," Jesse continued, "it wouldn't be hard at all. We could rig the flames with some filmy fabric in just the right colors and a few well-placed fans. It'd be epic, actually."

"Epic," Dylan echoed. "Don't people usually use that word in front of the noun *disaster*?"

Jesse frowned. "Pay no attention to Mr. Wet Blanket over there. We'll respect your watercraft, McDonald. And it will be *epic* in the best sense of the word."

"Definitely," Wally chimed in. Even Yorky looked as if he'd go for it.

Dylan looked over at Chad, who could usually be counted upon to bring a note of caution to any plan, but even he had a hint of a smile.

"We'd be sure to win. No one else could come close to an idea like that." Would Chad be so quick to endorse all this if the plan involved that truck he loved so much?

Then again, Dylan sighed, hadn't he just bemoaned his loss of fun to God in his morning prayer time? Maybe the answer involved a step out of his comfort zone like this—as long as the business didn't suffer.

"Everyone will be expecting us to trick the *High Tide* out to look like a fire truck—you know they will. This will be so much better." Jesse had already grabbed a sheet of paper from the shelf behind him and started sketching.

"We'd have to swear Charlotte and Abby to secrecy on the flame part," Chad advised. Dylan thought swearing Abby Reed to secrecy on anything was a sketchy proposition. Only Chad's wife, Jeannie, was Abby's best friend, so if anyone had the leverage to silence Abby, it would be the Owenses.

Jesse's pen was flying furiously over the paper. "The fact that we'd have to build it here and install it the night before just makes the surprise that much easier to pull off. I tell you, it's perfect."

Dylan wiped his hands down his face and tried not to panic at the notion that every part of his life was being pulled into this crazy event. "Well…"

"Come on." Wally stared at him. "This is brilliant. You're the chair of this thing—it'd look bad if you didn't have the best float."

Dylan had a last-minute reservation hit him. "It'll look rigged if we win, won't it?"

Jesse sat back in his chair. "Not if we deserve it. And believe me, we will." He gave Dylan a sideways look. "It will be awesome publicity for your business. And you need a project. You've got too much free time, dude." Jesse stopped just short of saying "You're a brokenhearted brood who needs his time occupied," but the tone of voice implied it loud and clear.

The free time crack wasn't true—at least not anymore. "Are you kidding? This thing is eating up every free moment I have. I never wanted to run this little circus—you know that." Perhaps it was best Chief Bradens wasn't in the room, or Dylan might have been tempted to direct that last line straight at him. Some days the chief's ideas of "personal development" on the part of his firefighters was a bit hard to take.

"Yeah, but the company is so pleasant." Jesse waggled his eyebrows.

"Not you three."

"No, your cochair. Cocaptain. Whatever you and Karla Kennedy are."

Dylan fought the urge to kick Jesse under the table, because now eyebrows were waggling all around. "Oh, yeah, her," and other such teasing comments rumbled around the table for an infuriating moment before Dylan stood up. "I think we're done here."

"Touchy, are we?" Yorky's smile was genuine but still annoying. "She's nice."

"She's going back to Chicago at the end of the summer." Dylan thought that comment would end the discussion, but as soon as the words left his mouth, he realized that simply implied that he and Karla had talked about it. Which wasn't true, but no one would believe it now even if he did deny it.

"End of summer's a long way away," Wally said. "She's kind of cute, if you like dark hair."

"And good coffee," Yorky added. "She made me some fancy drink the other day that was delicious. A 'macarooni' something."

Dylan laughed. "A macchiato?"

Yorky pointed a finger. "Yeah, that. Couldn't believe how much I liked it. Now, I wouldn't drink one every day—" his chest puffed up "—but it was my birthday and she offered to make me something special with my doughnut."

A chorus of "aww"s rang around the table. Yorky was a big guy but as soft as they came. He'd gotten his name from the tiny, delicate Yorkshire terrier his wife had bought. The husky fireman adored the little yippy thing but would never admit it. That made the third fireman Karla had won over this week. "Keep that up and we're going to have to ask Chief to put in one of those fancy espresso machines in the kitchen."

"Not on your life," came Chief Bradens's voice from the doorway. "This is a root beer firehouse, and that is not open to negotiation." Gordon Falls had a company that made outstanding root beer, and thanks to a close call with some burning equipment a decade ago, the firehouse had a continual free supply of the soda pop. The GFVFD drank root beer, period—no other soft drink was permitted. The only change to that decade-old setup had been the addition of diet root beer at JJ Cushman's request.

"I like going over to Karl's anyway." Jesse folded up his notes and tucked them in his shirt pocket. "I'd get tired of looking at your ugly mugs over coffee every day."

The group broke up, the meeting's goal evidently achieved, although Dylan couldn't remember actually saying "yes" to the grand scheme.

Jesse caught up with him in the hallway. "Hey, you are okay with all this, aren't you?"

Dylan was pleased someone even bothered to ask. "I suppose so. If you build it. I need that boat to live through the night, you know?"

"Not to worry, pal. I'll keep her safe." After a second he added, "You said business was going okay. That still true?" Jesse was in the beginning stages of launching his own home renovation business, so they had often talked shop.

"It's—" Dylan reached for the right word "—tight. The Coffee Catch thing is helping to perk up business—pun intended."

Jesse shook his head. "I know those loan payment schedules can keep a guy up at night. Your plan is solid. I know that, you know that. As a matter of fact, I was thinking about getting the guys to go in together on a charter to celebrate the chief's birthday next month."

Dylan was glad to hear that. He'd secretly worried that his friends and coworkers would pitch for free fishing trips now that he had all the equipment. Someday he could do things like that, but certainly not now. Just this morning he said a prayer of thanks that the Gordon Falls Community Church Knitting Circle had booked their own trip for this Wednesday—something about trying out hooks other than crochet hooks. "I think Chief Bradens would get a kick out of that."

"Shoot me an email with the dates you have open after the anniversary celebration is over. Coffee Catch included, of course."

Dylan grinned. "Of course."

Jesse's wide grin turned rather conspiratorial and he bumped a shoulder with Dylan as they walked down the hall. "So, how's it really going with your cochair?"

"What's that supposed to mean?"

"It's been nearly a week since you took her out fishing and I've yet to hear the details. How'd it go?"

Dylan didn't like where this was heading. "Everyone knows the details. She caught a huge fish."

Jesse bumped his shoulder again. "I'm talking about the other part. You know…the spending time out on the water with a clever, beautiful woman part."

Dylan stopped walking. "Oh, no, you don't. I'm not getting into this with you."

"That's fine by me, as long as you get into

it with *her.* She's perfect for you. You know that, don't you?"

It was time to shut this down. "Look, this is not happening. She is not perfect for me, and even if she was, I'm pretty sure she isn't interested."

"Could have fooled me. I heard about the two of you having breakfast at Karl's."

An irritating little voice yelled "I told you so!" from the back of Dylan's brain. "Eating eggs with a member of the opposite sex does not constitute the launch of a romantic entanglement. As a matter of fact, it was a committee chair meeting."

Jesse shrugged. "Yorky said she looked entangled."

"Why is Yorky—why is anyone, for that matter— watching me eat breakfast?" Dylan yanked the boat parade float sign-up sheet down from the firehouse bulletin board. He stared his friend straight in the eye, giving his words all the weight he could muster. "I am not her type. When you hear her talk about her plans for a snazzy city life, it doesn't take a rocket scientist to see she's looking for a shirt-and-tie guy. And that is not me."

It would have been nice if that shut Jesse up, but Dylan wasn't that fortunate. "Did the lady actually say that, or is that just Yvonne whispering in your ear?"

Some days Jesse's pushy nature was a useful trait. Today wasn't one of them. "Knock it off, Sykes. Now." He stuffed the sign-up sheet in his pocket and stomped out of the building before he had to listen to any more of his friend's nonsense.

Sunday afternoon, Karla spread the document she'd printed out from the Clifton on the kitchen table in the flat above Karl's. Dad had come over after church to fix the medicine cabinet hinge. He walked into the kitchen as he wiped the grease from his hands, stared over her shoulder. "So this is the program, huh?"

"A year stint at Perk. I can hardly wait. Dad, you should see the equipment they have there. The espresso machine alone costs more than my car."

Dad scanned the long list of bullet points outlining her responsibilities. "Sounds like a meal ticket. Any hotel in the world would hire you after this."

Her father still wasn't sold on the idea of her going into business for herself quite so soon. She knew her father recognized the apprenticeship at Perk for the prime opportunity it was, but she also realized he liked it even more as a stopgap to her moving forward with Rooster's.

"I don't want to work at a hotel, Dad. Rooster's is still my future. This will just be a fabulous stepping stone. I can look at spaces and get things set up while I'm working at Perk."

"When are you going to tell Grandpa?"

Karla leaned back in her chair and sighed. That was the real question, wasn't it? "Soon."

Dad sat down at the table. "He still thinks you're staying the whole summer, and this job starts in three weeks. You can't keep it from him for much longer."

"It'll make him so sad. He talks to me like I'm going to be here forever."

"I know." Her Dad had once been the target of Grandpa's "work at Karl's" pressure campaign. She never really thought she'd find herself in those shoes. "But that should be his problem, not yours. I have faith you'll find a way to tell him that won't hurt too much."

Karla wasn't so sure that was true. The wedge Dad's refusal had driven between him and Grandpa was still there, and it had been years. If the next generation of Kennedys inflicted the same wound, Karla was sure it would hurt even more. And that's what made this so hard. She fingered the papers. "This is what I'm supposed to do. I'm glad to help out here and all, but it's not my future. The Perk internship just proves to me that God is lining things up for me to launch Rooster's someday."

"So help Grandpa see it that way." He sighed. "I know I hurt him by going my own direction, but it was the right thing to do. That's why I think it's so important that you go in yours."

Karla decided to switch the topic. "There's still the problem of Karl's. Grandpa thinks he can go back to running the shop, but I don't think he can. It's a lot of work, even for me. How do we get him to come around on this and hire someone else?"

Dad folded his hands. "I think Dad knows— on some level, at least—that it's beyond him. He's just not ready to admit it. Hiring anyone to come in is a big leap for him, and hiring someone whose last name isn't Kennedy is an enormous leap. I think it's just that having you behind the counter has brought up old wishes, old dreams he had for the place. And the fact that he's just plain…old." One corner of Dad's mouth turned up in a wistful smile. "That's never easy for any of us to swallow."

Karla gathered the papers and put them back in a folder she'd proudly marked "Perk."

She needed to spend some serious time asking God's guidance on how to talk to the old man. "I love Grandpa. How do I tell him this without hurting him?"

Dad put his hand atop hers. "I'm not sure you can. But you can't let that stop you from moving forward with your own life. I went my own way, and while I won't say it was smooth sailing, I never regretted it. You've stepped in to help when you were needed, and now it's time to seize this great opportunity God's laid in front of you. You have to trust it will all work out." He squeezed her hand. "Eventually, if not at first." He straightened up, blew out a breath and changed the subject. "That Coffee Catch idea seems to be really catching on for Dylan. Who's up next?"

Karla laughed. "Oh, you'll love this one."

"Really? Who is it?"

"The Gordon Falls Community Church Knitting Circle."

Dad's jaw dropped. "What?"

"You know Violet. She's decided it shouldn't be just for tourists, that all the locals should help support Dylan's new business. So evidently all the women pooled their money and they're going fishing instead of knitting for their next meeting. It's hysterical, when you think of it."

"Aren't you part of that group?"

"Oh, they invited me. And I thought about it, but I think it's best to keep business and pleasure from mixing on this one." She slid her Perk file into her backpack alongside her textbooks. "I need to be at Karl's in order to make their drinks. Besides, it'd be a tight fit with all those women, Dylan and me."

"I don't know. You landed a pretty big fish last time you went out with him on that boat." Dad rubbed his stomach. "I'm hungry."

She waved her father away. "Very funny. No, I think I'll take a pass and just have their coffee waiting."

"Suit yourself. But it sounds like you might be missing out on some fun."

Chapter Ten

Knock. Knock. Knock-knock-knock. "Karla?"

Karla put down her hairbrush. Karl's wasn't due to open for another two hours; there was no reason for someone to be banging on her door.

"Karla, you're up, aren't you? I saw the light on. Are you decent?" A woman's voice whispered loudly on the other side of her door.

Yawning, Karla peered through the peephole to see Violet Sharpton in a windbreaker and some odd bucket hat that looked like it belonged on a…fisherman. That's right; it was Wednesday—the day of the Knitting Circle's Coffee Catch. She pulled open the door.

"You're coming with us," Violet declared, swooping into the room.

"Um…thanks, but I really have to get the shop open."

Violet went to Karla's closet door and pulled it open. "You'll want a jacket or something—it's still a bit chilly out there with the sun barely up."

The sun barely up, yes. All the more reason to... "Violet, why are you here?"

"Marge's arthritis is acting up again so now we have an empty space all paid for. You're a member of our group now—you should come. Melba can't bring Maria—she's too small for this sort of thing. Charlotte's already coming, so that leaves you."

Violet began filing through the hangers in Karla's closet, evidently looking for suitable outerwear. She turned, gave Karla's current clothing—perfectly presentable jeans and a T-shirt—a once-over, then plucked a Chicago Culinary School zip-front sweatshirt from the back of Karla's sofa and held it out. "Change into some sneakers and you'll be all set. Tina wants to see if she can catch one bigger than your champion fish, and you know how Tina gets."

She did not know how Tina got. She did not have time to go fishing this morning. "The shop..."

"I talked Karl and Emily into handling the morning crowd. And you can just make our spiffy coffees when we get in. No one's in any rush." Violet checked her watch. "Except us. Come on, we shove off in fifteen minutes. Captain McDonald said to be right on time."

Karla parked a hand on one hip. "Grandpa is not supposed to be working the shop. You know that."

"Of course, that's what the doctors say." She began rooting through a selection of headbands Karla kept in a bowl on a hallway table. "But he's going stir-crazy back at his house. Besides, I found him a stool to set behind the counter. He said 'yes' in a heartbeat, and Emily was happy to drive him in. Your father will meet Karl at the shop in an hour or two just in case he gets tired." She selected a red headband—the one Karla was intending to wear this morning, oddly enough—and held it out.

Karla narrowed her eyes as she took the headband from Violet. "So Dad's okay with this?"

"Well, I think he'd rather have slept in for another hour, but..."

Karla affixed the headband in the mirror, then stopped herself as soon as she realized she was obediently reaching for her sneakers. How did Violet Sharpton do that to people? "This is..."

"The best thing for everyone. Karl needs

this. You need a break. Dylan needs the business. Really, what kind of community are we if we don't support our own?" She planted her hands on her hips. "Oh, don't look at me like that! Karl's just going to work the register, that's all. I told him it's practice for his grand return…whenever that ends up being." Violet started for the door, then turned back. "Comb the back of your hair, child. It's wild all over the place."

Karla felt her mouth sag open. "I was just doing that." She was glad she was already showered and had her makeup on for the day—Violet looked as if she would have yanked her out in her pajamas in another second. She shook her head in disbelief, but not before grabbing at the comb sitting next to the bowl of headbands and tucking it into her jeans pocket while smoothing the back of her hair with her other hand.

"Have you brushed your teeth?" Violet peered at her.

"Of course I have." Karla tried not to grind the answer out through said teeth.

"Good—I would have waited for that, but we can get going."

"Why do you or the fish care about my grooming habits anyway?"

Violet blinked like a caffeinated owl. "Well, not *the fish*."

The knitting circle didn't have a dress code that she had ever known... Wait a minute. "Violet..." Karla said slowly, the arc of the woman's plan coming into view. "Oh, no. Stop that right now."

A sugar-sweet smile spread across Violet's face. "Stop what? Come on, dear, we need to go." She tucked Karla's hand into her elbow and ushered her out the door.

Karla yanked her hand free, needing to both slow things down and to lock her apartment door. "Stop pairing me off with Dylan McDonald!"

"Whatever gave you that idea?" Violet's hand went to her chest in the worst attempt at a "who, me?" Karla had ever seen. "The knitting circle is going fishing. You're in the knitting circle. There's no more to it than that."

There was loads more to it than that. All of this was getting out of hand. Karla fought back with the only thing she could think of. "You've got eyes for my grandfather." She wasn't quite sure why that made any sense as a deterrent to her current "kidnapping," but she hadn't even been able to finish her first cup of coffee yet this morning.

At first she was delighted to see that stop

Violet in her tracks, but the assessment proved premature. The senior citizen touched her elbow tenderly. "Well of course I do, sweetheart. I think your grandfather is the cat's pajamas." Her eyes took on a devious twinkle. "He's a grand kisser, that Karl."

Karla fell against the wall, hand on her forehead. "You've *kissed* Grandpa?"

Violet used this opportunity to zip up Karla's hooded sweatshirt as if she were a five-year-old being shipped off to kindergarten. "You needn't look so shocked. It's the twenty-first century and we're both consenting adults."

"Does Dad know?" Karla gawked as she returned her zipper to its original low position.

"Oh, I'd never tell him. That one's on Karl." Violet turned toward the stairwell that led to Tyler Street. "We really do need to get a move on."

If Violet Sharpton set out to share the one fact guaranteed to get Karla to follow her wherever she went for the next hour, she'd succeeded. She trailed the woman down the stairs, two dozen questions fighting for priority in her head. *How? When? Why?*

Why not? Was it really such an awful thing that Karl Kennedy had found love again in life? Hadn't she suspected the same thing weeks ago?

"How long?" she managed to spurt out as they pushed out the door at the bottom of the stairs.

"About two weeks ago," Violet trotted down Tyler Street in the direction of the boat docks as if the two of them were discussing the weather or sharing a new cake recipe. She threw a sparkling glance back at Karla. "Of course, that pot's been simmering for nearly a year now. Takes men longer to catch on to these sorts of things, don't you think?"

"I wouldn't know."

Violet produced a tin of mints from her handbag and offered one to Karla. "Well, and right there's your problem. What is it they say in that song from *Hello, Dolly!*? Something about Mother Nature needing a little help?"

Karla had seen the movie once back in high school, but she remembered enough to draw a striking comparison between the meddling Dolly and the woman currently dragging her toward a fishing boat. "Violet, I don't need your—" she struggled for a polite term "—help on this."

"Nonsense. I've seen the way he looks at you. For that matter, I've seen the way you look at him. And for crying out loud, I've seen the way he looks, period. What's more of a hottie than a fireman? That's the word you kids use now, isn't it?"

Karla hadn't used the term since high school, but that was beside the point. "Sure, he's nice looking." She would not bring herself to use the word *hottie* in front of Violet, although she wasn't blind to Dylan's handsome features. "But the timing's way off here. He's committed to Gordon Falls and I'm…" *Leaving in a little over two weeks.* She couldn't say it. Certainly not to Violet if she and Karl were so close. She was going to have to tell Grandpa soon. Really soon. "My plans don't really include living here."

"Oh, I've heard all about your highbrow breakfast spot plans. I like a woman determined to make her way in the world. But I ask you…" She turned the last corner to wave enthusiastically at the rest of the knitting circle gathered with Dylan on the dock. A cheer went up and Violet pumped her fist victoriously in the air, making Karla feel like some kind of contest prize. "What's the point of any success if there isn't someone to share it with?"

Karla couldn't think of any response except an exasperated groan.

* * *

There had been a regrettable ten-second stretch where Dylan thought this was a good idea. Unfortunately, by the time those ten seconds were up, Violet Sharpton was already headed down the road with her cell phone to her ear. Now, as he watched her walk up to the docks with a decidedly befuddled and not-exactly-awake Karla in tow, he couldn't possibly weigh in on the merits of the plan.

He'd be lying to himself if he said he didn't find her fascinating before, in a clever, woman-going-places kind of way. Her sleek hair, city clothes, the rather exotic way she smelled, even the sophistication of her makeup appealed to him in a way that Gordon Falls' "girl next door" types never had. He'd always gone for the sophisticated women—that wasn't much of a surprise, even if it might have been his downfall.

What *was* a surprise was how the sight of a barely up-and-running Karla charmed him. Somehow, in their earlier fishing trip, she'd still managed to look pulled together. Drowsy, but still her unique brand of low-key stylish. Now, she looked as if Violet had dragged her out of bed. The red headband she wore made the indigo in her eyes pop against her pale skin, even with her hair all sticking up in the back as if she'd slept on it wrong. And the cooking school sweatshirt? It gave her an unkempt, almost-intimate quality that grew rocks in his stomach. *Adorable* was for puppies, baby ducks and the like, but he couldn't come up with another word. Under any other circumstances, the hum in his gut might have had him leaning against the boat rail, chin in his hand, staring at her. He'd have to get that impulse under control before these knitting grandmothers took that ball of yarn and ran with it.

"And good morning to you," Charlotte Taylor teased, holding out a tin mug of coffee from Dylan's onboard thermos. Charlotte was no grandmother—she was going to be Jesse Sykes's bride in a few months if Jesse went ahead with his plans to pop the question. At least he wouldn't be the only one on the boat in his twenties; on some excursions he felt like the baby of the bunch.

Karla stood on the dock with an amused scowl. "Seems I've been kidnapped to go fishing."

"There are worse fates," Jeannie Owens consoled. "And I brought chocolate." Since Jeannie owned the town candy shop, Dylan suspected she'd be packing confections for the trip. She'd already deposited a small bag of goodies in his captain's chair.

Karla eyed Dylan. "Were you in on this?"

"Absolutely not." He was glad he didn't have to hedge on that point. Would he have been glad to know she was coming? Yes. A large part of him yearned to get her back out on the river with him—it had been the most fun he'd had in months. As it was, it felt like that moment on a middle school playground where a herd of boys pushes one poor guy up toward an embarrassed middle school girl flanked by a gaggle of conniving friends. He shrugged at Karla. "Still, a day off's a day off, right?"

The ladies sent up a chorus of agreement as they boarded. If he could manage to stay in control of the situation, this still had a shot at being fun. Only that was a whopping "if" with this crowd.

Imagine his surprise when the women settled into their seats quickly to leave the only open seat for Karla up next to him. He kept his eyes on the dock lines rather than reveal how amusing he found the flush in her cheeks. Who knew he'd find the pink shade of her lips even more attractive than the alluring burgundy lip gloss she normally wore?

"Where are we headed?" she asked, her

hair still fluttering across her face despite the headband. It was a sensible question, but her eyes flashed an "I have no idea what's going on here" panic. He knew the sensation—it was like being cornered, only a whole lot nicer than that.

"They all want to go where you landed your big fish."

"That's right," called Tina from her place at the back of the boat. "We want to come home with big trophy fish, too. Show those men how well a lady can land a whopper." A chorus of encouragement piped up around the boat. Dylan said a silent prayer for fishing favor—he definitely didn't want to bring these women home empty-handed after they'd been so supportive of him. Only he couldn't quite say if this was commercial support or just the most creative bit of social meddling he'd ever seen.

Pulling into the cove where he'd spent that enjoyable morning with Karla, Dylan dropped anchor and began to get out the poles. "Okay, ladies, how many of you have fished before?"

All hands went up. Good. With a full boat, it was better not to have first-timers. He pulled the tub of bait from the cooler. "You can all bait your own hooks?" Again, all affirmatives—even Karla, who'd surprised him by mastering the art on their last trip. He gave them a few other instructions, finding himself more and more entertained at the constant words of encouragement that flowed back and forth between the women. Men were, for the most part, much more competitive when they fished.

The ladies sorted themselves out around the back of the boat, not-too-subtly leaving the bow for Dylan and Karla.

"Do you think they're up to something?" Dylan finally chuckled, thinking it was better to own up to things than opt for denial.

"Gosh, whatever gave you that idea?" Karla's eyes grew wide in mock astonishment.

"They're just having a bit of fun, you know." He shot a glance back at the group, who were chatting away between casting lines or throwing an occasional look at him and Karla with whispered commentary. "Harmless, mostly." Then, just to take the edge off, he said, "Maybe I should tango with you up here—you know, something just to show them up."

It was a terrible idea, but he couldn't ignore that there was a part of him that wanted to pursue Karla. It was just that there were too many other parts of him ready to shut down that idea for the dead-end prospect that it was.

"You know how to tango?"

He regretted the slip. "I took classes. Yvonne thought it was trendy and liked to show off at parties." His brain concocted the split-second image of Karla's dark hair trailing down as he took her into a low dip—the exact opposite of Yvonne's tight, sophisticated bun of blond hair—and he swallowed more coffee to clear his head. He leaned starboard for a second, knowing it would rock the boat a bit. "Nautical tango. Bad idea. One of us would end up swimming."

"If not both of us." Karla selected a worm, dangling it up. "Help me pick a loser here."

"A what?"

"Look," she edged closer, lowering her voice, "the last thing I need is to catch another big fish today. Someone else needs to land in the limelight this morning, if you know what I mean. Gordon Falls' champion female fisherman should be someone who is staying longer than one season, don't you think?"

He liked that she thought of the others, even after they'd abducted her and played dockside matchmaker. Still, was she going out of her way to remind him that her time in Gordon Falls was coming to an end? He leaned in and took the worm from her, slyly returning it to the bait container. "Don't bait your hook at all. Just drop it in the water bare. I'll cover for you."

"Oooh!" came an excited squeal from the back of the boat. "I've got one!"

"See?" Dylan found himself smiling at her. "My plan's working already."

By the time they'd finished their morning expedition, the women had become suspicious of Karla's lack of success. They teased her about "letting Tina win," especially when Tina landed a nice big bluegill that should meet her requirement for a good showing with the menfolk. In fact, Karla was the only person not to pull in several nice fish, and she didn't seem to mind her empty haul one bit.

"I had fun," she said as Dylan helped her climb out of the boat. "Unexpected, way-too-early fun, but fun just the same."

"Now you can talk me up to all your city friends." Dylan had meant it to sound casual, but it put a sore punctuation on the end of what had been a really enjoyable morning. For all the growing attraction he felt for Karla, nothing changed the fact that she'd be moving 160 miles away in a matter of weeks. She'd even told him her secret about the incredible internship she'd been offered—how on earth could he hope to compete with that kind of opportunity? Only a jerk would try to draw a smart woman away from such a bright future.

As for right now, the pressure was on. They had two weeks to finish plans for the celebration and concoct the surprise handoff to Violet and Karl—and speaking of surprises! When Karla confided what she'd learned about the two seniors, Dylan nearly dropped his pole into the river.

It was the last thing he needed; another Gordon Falls man finding true love. Some days small towns were just too small.

Chapter Eleven

"Come here, Karla. I don't think I've ever shown you this." Grandpa methodically worked his way through the stock room at the back of the coffee shop to the little alcove where he kept a small desk and a drawer of files. He wasn't here in a working capacity today—he hadn't yet officially returned—but was just stopping by for a visit.

She followed her grandfather to the back office, remembering how much she'd loved sitting with him back here when she was little—it was like a secret hiding place. Even when he hadn't been in the shop in weeks, no one sat at the desk in his absence; it was Karl's space and probably always would be. A little knot rose in her throat as she watched him ease himself carefully into the old chair. The day of "Karl's without Karl" was coming. It was probably nearer than anyone cared to admit. Karla couldn't stand the thought, and yet it was clear to everyone—except Grandpa—that it was too much for him to handle alone. It made it so much harder to tell him she was leaving.

She edged past a box of paper napkins to join him in the cluttered little corner. "What did you want to show me, Grandpa?"

He pointed to a framed dollar bill hanging on the wall. It wasn't an unusual thing—many restaurants and lots of businesses framed their first transaction and hung it on the wall. "I've seen this before. It's your first dollar, I know."

Grandpa lifted the small black frame from its place on the wall. Karla wasn't that surprised to see a faded spot in its place—the thing had been hanging there for years. "Yes, but read the inscription."

There, in faded ballpoint pen, were the words *Best Wishes, Oscar*.

"Oscar was your first customer?" It was hard to envision him wishing anyone well.

"He was different back then. We were good friends." Regret softened Grandpa's eyes and his words. Suddenly it was easier to see why he put up with the sour-faced grocer and kept his coffee at a ridiculous price.

She sat down on a box, staring at the words. "What happened?"

"He was married, you know. He and his wife, Alice, were the best of friends with your grandmother and I. Did all kinds of stuff together. Alice was your father's godmother. We had grand times."

Karla looked up. "And then?"

"Oscar opened the store a year before I opened this place. We'd spend endless hours plotting and planning our little town empires." He chuckled. "Oh, we had such dreams— Oscar more than me. He wanted to own a chain of grocery stores up and down the river. I think he would, too, if it hadn't been for Alice."

"Alice?"

"Oscar worked hard. Long hours. Alice was pregnant, so she mostly stayed home. Your grandmother would help her out, keep her company and such, seeing how Oscar was gone so much…" Grandpa drew a deep breath, then went on. "One night Oscar was at the store during a big storm, worried about the new roof he'd just put on. Alice was home, but she got nervous so she decided to drive to the store and spend the night there with him rather than being home alone. That was back when Tyler Street ran down right close to the river."

There was a levee now between Tyler Street and the river, and for good reason. Karla felt her hand stray to her throat. "No."

"She missed the turn and the car slid into the river. Current took it almost a hundred yards they say, before it lodged under the bridge. They wanted to put a plaque there, but Oscar wouldn't let them. Never seen a man come unglued like that, and I hope to never again."

Suddenly Grandpa's coffee discount seemed like a quiet kindness. Only they never spoke like the old friends Grandpa made them out to be. "That's so sad."

"Margaret and I tried to be there for him, to help him along, but it was as if our happiness just made his tragedy worse. Three's hard to manage comfortably, you know? By the time Margaret passed away, there'd been too much water under the bridge—literally—to pick up the friendship. He comes in for breakfast, I serve him coffee and listen to him complain."

Grandpa let out an enormous sigh. "And I remember this dollar back here and why I'm glad I never wanted to own a chain of restaurants." He returned the dollar to its place on the wall, one finger touching the edge of the frame. Karla noticed one corner was worn down, as if he touched it often.

Sadness pinched her heart and a lump rose to her throat. How easily she'd dismissed Oscar as just a grouch without wondering what had soured him so. She looked back at her grandfather. "Why did you want me to know this now?"

Grandpa's hand moved from the frame to clasp her own hand. "Because I know you have big dreams. And big dreams are great things, but only if you don't let them get in the way of what really matters. Don't let anyone tell you your dreams are too big, but don't let your plans get so big that they don't leave room in your life for someone, either."

Did he know? Had Dad told him? She looked at a yellowed newspaper clipping on the wall above the dollar. Brittle around the edges, it showed a grinning Karl and Margaret Kennedy behind the cash register, a tenth anniversary special written on the chalkboard behind them. Karla felt tears sting her eyes. "You and Grandma made a great team."

"I think it's time you became part of that team, Karla. You've done a fine job here. A fine job. That's made me realize it might be time for me to start letting go. Maybe do more fishing. Let the next generation of Kennedys show how they can do."

Karla thought her heart would twist in half.

She couldn't put it off any longer. "I've loved working here, Grandpa—really I have." She knew her tone conveyed what she was going to say next, and the sight of the glow leaving his eyes broke her heart. "But this is your dream. It's not mine."

He said nothing, just slowly returned his gaze to the framed dollar on the wall. He touched the corner with his finger again, and the gesture had the feel of a goodbye. Karla's throat tightened and tears stung her eyes. "You've heard me talk about Rooster's, Grandpa. That's my dream." She put her hand on his, but he did not turn his palm over to clasp her hand the way he usually did. "I'm hoping Rooster's leads me to someone as good for me as Grandma was for you."

"You and that chicken place." That's what he'd taken to calling her plans. It was her fault that out of pity, she'd always couched her plans for Rooster's as something far-off and long-term.

"Yeah," she said, wiping one eye. "Me and that chicken place. I have a great internship at a fancy hotel in Chicago that starts on July 16. I'll need to be back in Chicago by then, Grandpa. It will open a lot of doors for me, but it will work because of everything I learned here."

"You've done so well here." Grandpa sounded dangerously close to pleading, twisting the knife in Karla's heart even further. "Even Oscar likes you."

She tried to laugh, but the threat of tears squelched the sound. "Gosh, you'd never know. I was thinking he found me a pretty poor substitution."

"That's the thing about some people. You have to look down past the parts everyone else sees. And if you can do that, well, then, that's a gift." Grandpa started to drag himself up out of the chair. "Everyone says they come here for the pie, but it's about how you look them in the eye. You remember that."

Karla hugged her grandfather tight. "When I open Rooster's, will you be my first dollar?"

The resignation in Grandpa's eyes pressed on her shoulder like a hundred pounds. He poked her nose the way he used to when she was a tiny girl swinging her legs at the shop counter while he made her a cherry cola, but it had such an air of farewell to it that tears slid down one cheek. "I'll be your first ten dollars." He held her at arm's length. "'Cause that's what one of your fancy coffee's gonna set me back, isn't it?"

"Nah," she replied, hugging him and pressing her wet cheek to his. "Yours will always be free." She nodded at the frame on the wall. "Except the first one, and that'll cost you a dollar. And an autograph."

She watched him make his way to the front of the shop, unable to follow him. Instead, she opened the back door that led out into the alleyway, sat down on the loading dock and quietly cried.

Dylan pushed the back door of the coffee shop open to find Karla sitting on the loading dock with her back to him. "Karl said you were out here."

She sniffed, straightened her shoulders and turned toward him with a weak wave. She'd been crying.

He moved to sit next to her. "What's wrong?"

She looked up with a deep breath, settling her shoulders. "I just told Grandpa I'm not taking over Karl's."

"But you've never been taking over Karl's. I thought he knew that."

"I think he knew that, too. I just finally had to come out and say it. That, and that I'm leaving on the sixteenth, if not before. It's been as if we've been in a little bubble pretending that isn't going to happen, and I just popped that bubble."

"You had to tell him."

She flapped her hand in the air as if to shoo away the fresh tears that appeared in her eyes. "I know that. I just didn't count on it being so hard. He looked so hurt."

"He had to know, and the sooner the better. It will get better from here, I think. He'll come around." He risked putting a hand on her shoulder. "We'll get him hopelessly busy with anniversary celebration tasks so he won't have time to pout." She looked like a change of subject would do her good. "How did the picnic planning go?"

She took the lead he offered. "Great. Everyone will be invited to picnic on the riverfront before the boats go by. Dellio's diner is going to cater fried chicken and all the fixings for the guys in the department, and Jeannie Owens is organizing a cake competition that the firemen will get to judge, so dessert's covered, too."

"Wow. You managed all that since Saturday?"

Karla managed a weak smile. "Chad took care of the picnic paperwork, Jeannie came up with the idea on her own and I sent Violet Sharpton down to Dellio's. No one says no to Vi."

"Don't we all know that."

An awkward silence fell between them. Dylan tried to think of more to say, but came up empty. "I can't go back out there," she moaned. "Not yet."

That gave him an idea. He hopped down off the loading dock. "No one's at the firehouse at the moment—why don't you come over for a few minutes to see something?"

"Um, sure." She seemed glad of the diversion.

"I'll have to swear you to secrecy, but I need someone to know this wasn't my idea."

They slipped out into the alleyway and across the street to the side door of the empty firehouse. He led her through a pair of hallways until they opened out to a shedlike structure in back of the firehouse. Sliding the bolt, Dylan opened the shed's double doors to reveal the workshop they'd used for the float construction. Four log cabin "walls" leaned against the side of the shed in various stages of construction. A set of plans and an artist's rendering done by Charlotte were tacked up on the wall.

She looked surprised. "This is the firehouse's float?"

"Yep. They're using my boat, but I didn't put them up to this."

Karla peered at a second sketch, one that showed the same log cabin consumed in flames. "Wait…you're setting your float on fire?"

"Not really." Dylan pointed to the mechanical detail on one of the drawings. "Jesse and Charlotte are rigging some kind of special effect with thin fabric and fans."

She glanced back at him, smirking in the sunlight coming in through the shed windows. He was glad to see some of the light come back to her eyes. "That's crazy. You know that, don't you?"

"Well, I think it's a bit overdone, yeah. But they're having fun, and it's not as if my boat's in any danger."

Karla peered back at the plans. "Are you sure about that?"

He laughed. "I trust Jesse. I wouldn't fight fires with him if I didn't. Or any of them. These guys always have my back. Always."

"It's nice to know there are still people like that in the world." She leaned against the wall, hugging her chest. "Why'd you start? With the firehouse, I mean?"

"I told you. I needed something bigger than me when I came here." He picked up one of the paper tube things stacked up against the wall and thumped it on the ground. "I suppose I needed somewhere to belong, silly as that sounds."

"I don't think that sounds silly at all." She waved her hand around the room. "Honestly, I think you'll win. I don't know about all the floats, but I haven't heard of anything as elaborate as this."

"That's just it—I don't want to win. The whole weekend's already about the firehouse, I don't think we should take over the parade as well when it's supposed to be a whole community thing."

She stared at him. "Why shouldn't you want to win the prize? I'd think the firehouse would consider its honor at stake here and go all out to win. I don't need to know that this wasn't your idea because it wouldn't bother me if it was."

"I'm not the grandstanding type. I just wanted you to know."

"Okay, point taken," she said. "You're going along with this for the good of the firehouse, but it wasn't your idea. Got it."

"Good." He turned toward the door.

"Dylan?"

"What?"

"Ambition isn't a bad thing, you know. Not if you hold it in balance."

He didn't answer.

Chapter Twelve

Karla sat at Max Jones's wedding reception the following Saturday night feeling sad, awkward and out of place. Why had she ever thought coming would be a good idea? She wasn't really part of this community; she'd only been invited as a courtesy to Grandpa. And right now, Karl was sulking.

The party should have proved a welcome distraction, but it wasn't. The love story between Max Jones and Heather Browning was a fabulous tale that should have made anyone happy—a young man in a wheelchair finding love with the local high school guidance counselor—yet she still felt a heavy weight pressing down on her.

The back deck of the Black Swan, one of Gordon Falls' nicer restaurants, had been transformed for the joyous couple. Max was a Karl's Koffee regular, despite all the accommodations it took for him to enter the shop using his wheelchair. Max was one of Grandpa's favorite "personal policies"; if Grandpa had to move you to another seat so that Max could use the only table that would accommodate his wheelchair, your coffee was on the house. Grandpa had scores of "personal policies"—they were part of what made Karl's the homey place it was. Could Perk achieve that kind of personal service? She'd want to find a way at Rooster's, that was sure.

Even though he hadn't looked her in the eye all night, Grandpa was trying to make the best of his first true social outing, shaking hands and shouting hello. Karla tried to cheer herself by watching everyone be so happy for two people who looked happier still. She finally managed to shed most of her doldrums by the time Max and Heather had their first dance. A pretty impressive feat since Max used a wheelchair. The tender moment left barely a dry eye in the house, Karla included.

The night's biggest surprise, however, was the sight of Dylan in full dress uniform. Max wasn't a fireman, but his sister JJ was, and evidently Max had "borrowed" the knees of the entire department to propose to Heather since he couldn't get down on one knee himself. To honor their role in the engagement, all the invited firemen—which was practically the entire department—wore their dress uniforms to the ceremony.

Karla didn't need anyone to point out how well the uniform suited Dylan—even though Violet, Tina, Marge and several other of the other knitting circle women went out of their way to do so. Karla's inclination had been correct: Dylan MacDonald was handsome in casual clothes, but he was downright stunning in formal attire. The navy of the uniform doubled the intensity of his eyes, and while she preferred his hair messy and just shaken out of a baseball cap, it gave him a whole other kind of appeal tamed and combed.

She did her best to stay on the other side of the gathering, but it was a lost cause. Karla wondered if Dylan could sense the unease in her expression—after all, she had told him on the fishing expedition that her departure would be soon. She could certainly see the tension in his broad shoulders. A wedding must be a hard thing to watch for a man who'd had his own near engagement go so painfully awry. They kept catching each other's eye from opposite sides of the happy crowd until, finally, just as Max and Heather were feeding each other slices of wedding cake, Dylan walked over to stand next to her.

"They look so happy." His voice was stretched tight with regret as he stared at the couple.

"Is it hard to watch?" She was sorry for the question, but there was no mistaking an edge of pain in Dylan's eyes. He said he'd been about to propose to Yvonne—surely he'd imagined what their wedding would have been like.

Dylan didn't speak, but simply nodded. Karla watched him clench his jaw, keenly aware of the wound Dylan still carried.

"Want to get some air?"

"Yeah." He snickered, realizing at the same moment she did that the comment was ludicrous on an outdoor patio. He tilted his head toward the riverbank. "Or water."

They walked in silence down toward the riverbank, hearing the boisterous party noises fade behind them to be absorbed in the quiet sounds of the river on a summer evening.

Dylan stuffed his hands in his uniform pockets. "Sorry about that."

She didn't think he had anything for which to apologize. "You're far from over her, huh?" Some things didn't go by practical timetables.

"Oh, no," came his quick reply, "I'm over

Yvonne. The only feelings left for her are—" he shook his head "—well, not terribly honorable, let's just leave it at that." The night was warm, and he undid the gold buttons that closed the dark double-breasted uniform jacket. "I don't quite know why that was so hard. I wasn't expecting that." He sat down on the low stone wall that faced the river, undoing the top button on his shirt and loosening his tie.

"Makes sense to me." She sat down close beside him, drawn in by his soft tone and somber mood. "Woulda, shoulda, coulda, you know?"

He cracked a forlorn smile. "I *shoulda* seen her for what she was, then I *coulda* left her alone and I *woulda* avoided all this hurt."

"Hey, we can't always see what's coming down the road."

He turned to her, moonlight casting his face into stark features. "Yeah, well look at you. You know just where you're going, are honest about it, and you're just about off on your way to get there." He pushed out a breath. "I just hope it lives up to your expectations." It wasn't sour grapes, more of a gentle warning.

"I've really liked being here," Karla felt compelled to say. "It's not where I belong, but I can see why Grandpa loves this place so much. Why you love it so much. I can see how it could become hard to leave."

He gave a low laugh. "You didn't think much like that when I first met you."

"Yeah, well, I wasn't cochair of the big anniversary bash and catcher of the town's prize fish back then." Karla kicked her feet out to cross her ankles in front of her, a bit surprised at the wave of affection that flooded over her as she remembered the fuss over that fish. "Serious résumé booster, the lot of it."

"Glad to know we enhanced your credentials." There was just the slightest edge to his words.

"It was more than that. You know it was."

He turned to look at her. "Was it?"

She owed him honesty, the knowledge that a woman could be straight with him. "This isn't the place for me. Everyone's wonderful, and I know what people are thinking. Goodness knows it's crystal clear what Grandpa was thinking, but it's not..." She couldn't find the words for what she wanted to say that didn't sound dismissive, or worse yet, city-snobbish.

"It's not Chicago," he finished for her. "Funny," he said sourly, "that's precisely why I love it." He straightened up, pulling his tie from his collar. "If I'd stayed, if we were sitting on a high-rise balcony in Chicago instead of on a stone wall in Gordon Falls, would we even know each other?"

That was easy to answer. "I hope so."

"That'd fit the Karla Kennedy master plan, wouldn't it?" He stood up off the wall and took a few steps away from her. "That wasn't fair. That was out of line." He turned back to stare at her. "Sore spot for me, you know?"

What wasn't fair was how emotionally raw, how honest and charming he looked washed in moonlight with that wounded grin on his face. He didn't belong on a high-rise balcony in Chicago and never would. He belonged right here. Was it so awful to admit that now just a small part of her did, too? "I'm glad I came."

"You did the right thing. You helped your family out in a tight spot."

"I'm glad I came for other reasons, too. I'm not sorry we met."

"You're just sorry we met *here*." He said it with a tone of regretful acceptance.

It was true. "Yes." The moment was tumbling toward something that wasn't smart for either of them. A closeness that would only make everything more difficult instead of easier. Half out of distraction, half out of curiosity, and because she knew she'd probably never get another chance to find out, Karla stood up and asked, "Hey, Captain McDonald, can you really tango, or was that just a fish tale?"

He laughed. "I most certainly can. In fact, I am the best Scottish tango dancer you will ever know."

Karla laid her sweater on the stone wall. "Prove it."

Karla looked at him with such a daring playfulness in her eyes. Dylan knew right then and there that he didn't want to play the victim anymore. Why not take that beautiful woman in his arms and slay all the bad memories Yvonne had dumped on him? How many times had Jesse told him to "snap out of it"? Right here, right now, was the first safe chance to do that. Things were destined not to work out between him and Karla—she wanted everything he'd left behind, and the timing couldn't be further off. This was one night, one chance to take back a piece of himself that Yvonne seemed to have stolen.

Dylan took off his uniform jacket and laid it on the stone wall. "You'd better mean that."

She put her hands on her hips, a feisty ball of challenge. "I most certainly do."

He looked around. "We don't have any music."

She wasn't going to let him get away that easily. "I have a smartphone."

He crossed his arms over his chest. "Oh, got a tango tune all cued up, do you?"

She held up her fingers in the universal "5 seconds" gesture, then rifled through her handbag for her phone and began tapping furiously. As she worked, her tongue stuck out just the tiniest bit, and his pulse kicked up a notch at the endearingly unconscious quirk. It seemed as if every time he was with her some little detail would add itself to the pile of things he liked about her. A smarter man would have stopped that pile from getting any more chances to grow, but it had been so long since he'd met any woman that made him even consider taking chances with his heart. Even stupid, doomed chances.

"Ha!" she proclaimed, setting the phone on the wall and punching a final button. "Technology for the win." The first strains of "La Cumparsita," that one song everyone thought of for tangos but only tango fans could name, wafted out into the night.

"Predictable, but it works." Dylan undid his cuff buttons and rolled up his sleeves.

She pulled back. "Too obvious?" Then, she got an idea. Honestly, the sight of that woman getting an idea was like a shot of espresso. Holding up a finger again, she darted back to the phone, tapped some more and began a low, playful laugh as the Proclaimers' "I'm Gonna Be" started up.

"A Scottish band, Mr. Scottish tango man."

A pop song? *That* pop song? "How on earth did you come up with that?"

She grinned. "I just typed 'Scottish tango songs' into the search engine."

"There are no Scottish tango songs."

She pointed to her phone. "Are you going to stand here and argue with the internet or are you going to deliver?"

The steady beat of the song filled the night air. He knew the song, knew the band, but hadn't *ever* thought of it in terms of a tango. Only as he stood there and counted out the rhythm, it worked. It actually fit in a weird, crazy way. Somehow, with that one offbeat suggestion, Karla Kennedy yanked all the hurt right out from underneath him. She was there, in a circle of lamplight, ready to hand an enormous chunk of his heart back to him with her outstretched hand.

He took her hand, feeling something zing through him as he did. "Do you even know how?"

She cocked her head to one side. "Can't be that hard."

"Oh, it's harder than it looks."

Her chin tipped up in defiance. He put his hand to her waist and counted out the beat, made easy by the pop song's powerful drumbeat. "Slow, slow, quick-quick slow."

Karla tripped twice, but he caught her, saving her from falling. By the end of the first verse she was following his lead, laughing when she goofed instead of getting frustrated the way Yvonne always would. For the first time in ages, the comparison didn't pinch; it freed him.

By the chorus, she was having fun. The combination of the rowdy Scottish pub song with a summer night tango somehow made it all new again. Karla had given him lots of gifts over these few weeks, but even if this was the last one, he'd walk away a happy man.

When the bridge came, a rousing burst of "da-da-da" nonsense syllables, Karla pulled away from him and began joyfully dancing around the makeshift dance floor, a ridiculous jig of waving arms that sent him doubled over laughing.

Laughing. How long had it been since he'd laughed like that? It swept the stale air from his lungs. When the verse returned, he pulled her back into the tango, indulgently staring into her eyes and holding her the tiniest bit closer. It would be okay, just for tonight. This felt like such a restoration. "Get ready," he said, sure his grin filled every part of his face.

"For what?"

"For this." With that he dipped her, enjoying the way her arms tightened around him as he pulled her off balance. It wasn't anything close to elegant, but it was spectacular in its own crazy way. He relished the way her hair swept around her face when he pulled her back up and spun her into a turn. When she missed a step and ended up with one foot tangled around his leg, he felt her laugh ripple over him until he laughed himself.

When the chorus came back around, he didn't let her leave him, but promptly picked her right up off the ground to spin her around until she threw her head back and shouted the lyrics right along with him.

He hadn't planned to kiss her. He shouldn't have, given the circumstances. But when he dipped her again and she stared up at him with those incredible ink-blue eyes, he couldn't have helped himself for all the world. She had all this joy and determination and energy and he just needed to taste it, to breathe it in and wake back up to a world where love didn't leave so many scars. To kiss a woman in a tango dip was the most romantic thing in the whole world, and tonight he wanted to give that to her.

Her hand slipped around his neck, and he could feel the instant when she chose to kiss him back, feel the sensible side of her fall away and indulge in the moment they were sharing. It was so much more than attraction, it was romance—that pure, heart-to-heart thing he was pretty sure he'd killed off. He took a deep breath as he kissed her, the scent of her and the summer night and his own heart beating again pouring over him in lush, sparkling waves.

He didn't even notice that the music had stopped; his own happiness was roaring in his ears. He was holding almost all her weight, tipped over as she was, but he felt none of it. He wasn't even sure he felt the ground under his own feet. As a matter of fact, when she made this little sound—this tiny, blissful mewling sound—it shot through him so fast he thought he might drop her. Only he didn't. He hung on tight, and she clung to him. The sensation was dazzling. Heart-stopping. Unforgettable. Really, really dangerous.

He pulled her back upright, restoring their vertical balance but feeling completely off-kilter in every other way. When she took the smallest step back, breathing as hard as he was, he felt the space between them too keenly. As if it were a mistake to be far from her.

And she was leaving. He'd known all along she was leaving, they'd talked about it on the *High Tide*, they'd even planned for it, but it suddenly felt all wrong. He could sit down right now and list a dozen reasons why he'd never want to pull her from her dream of Rooster's in Chicago, and still gladly defy all of them for another moment like the one he'd just had. Not exactly an honorable sentiment, was it?

Karla hugged herself, cheeks bright pink, eyes wide, lips that memorable shade of burgundy he could never quite get out of his head. A lock of her hair—dark and glossy in the lamplight—fell across her cheek, and he swallowed the urge to tuck it behind her ear. "Um...wow." Her voice held the startled spark he currently felt igniting in his chest.

"Yeah." *Should I apologize?* He couldn't genuinely do it—he couldn't bring himself to regret kissing her. It'd been such a gift to kiss her and feel that way again.

"So…what do we do about *that*?" She sat down on the wall, and he wondered if she felt as dizzy as he did.

He sat down next to her. Not touching her, but still close. "I'm not sure I know." He looked at her, glad she held his gaze. "Do we have to do anything about it?"

"I need to leave. You need to stay here. That kind of calls for something to be done, doesn't it?"

Suddenly it was important to say, "I'm not sorry I kissed you. Not at all. It was—" having started, he now found he had no idea how to finish "—amazing. And I have to tell you, I wasn't sure I could do amazing ever again."

She knit her fingers together. "It's all wrong, you know? All the details, the circumstance, the timing. It's all off. Mixed-up."

He shrugged. "I thought it all lined up perfectly with Yvonne, and look what happened. I don't think you can go by how easy it feels."

She stared at the river. "This part feels easy. I mean not the tango—you're right, that's much harder than it looks—but this part. Only there are other pieces that don't fit together." She turned to look at him. "Pieces I'm not ready to give up."

"And you shouldn't." Much as he wanted to hit the pause button on this summer, to freeze these moments right where they were, he didn't want her to stop being the tenacious woman determined to open her own place. "You're great at Karl's, but you're supposed to be more than just your grandfather's replacement. I'd never want to keep you here." He sighed. "And I'd never want to go back. Not to Chicago."

"It's not like we can meet in Rockford," she mused, citing the city roughly halfway between Chicago and Gordon Falls.

He knew, even as she said it, that there wasn't a compromise to be had here. Feeling the possibility slip sadly between his fingers, he leaned over and kissed her gently again. "So that's what you'll be."

"What?" she said, blinking up at him, breaking off a piece of his heart that had just come back to life.

He tucked that wayward strand of hair back behind her ear. "The one that got away."

Chapter Thirteen

"McDonald, you're an idiot." Jesse glared at Dylan over the top of the fire truck as they were washing it Monday afternoon.

"I knew you'd say that." Already sorry he had given in to his friend's relentless demands to know what happened after he and Karla were seen leaving the wedding reception together, Dylan braced for a lecture.

"She's perfect for you." Jesse began working a rag around a fixture as if it fed the words. "She's smart, she's pretty, she catches monster fish on your boat, she makes coffee that keeps your customers happy, and you're hooked on her. Even I can see it. For crying out loud, half the town can see it."

Dylan tossed a rag into the sudsy bucket at his feet. While Jesse was known to exaggerate facts as easily as he breathed, this was precisely why he hesitated leaving the reception with Karla. Tongues in Gordon Falls wagged at even the slightest encouragement. If the wedding festivities hadn't been grating on his nerves so much, he would have never left with Karla, never opened her to that kind of small-town speculation. Still, he couldn't bring himself to regret the moments he'd shared with her two nights ago out on the riverbank. The "Scottish tango song" had been running through his mind nonstop for the past forty-eight hours. "Half the town? Or just Violet and her buddies?"

"Oh, yeah, the kidnapping. I suppose the pump was primed long before Hot Wheels tied the knot, huh?" Jesse was referring to Max Jones's nickname, a favorite of Violet's and Karl's and a few other Gordon Falls residents. Jesse leaned on one elbow on top of the truck. "It's not such a big deal, Dylan. I mean, it's not like you were kids kissing out back behind the school dance or anything."

Dylan froze, even though he told his limbs not to give anything away. He'd deliberately left the kiss out, hoping the spontaneous dance would be enough to satisfy Sykes's relentless curiosity.

Too late. Jesse practically climbed up the truck to point a finger at him. "You did! You kissed her, didn't you? It's all over your face, buddy." He laughed, annoyingly pleased. "Oh, man, she's even better for you than I thought." He planted his chin in one hand, ready for a long story. "And?"

Dylan was not of the "kiss and tell" variety. He didn't want to say anything at all—the wonder of that kiss was still working its way through his system. He didn't know himself yet what it all meant, and he certainly wasn't in the mood to work it out with the likes of Jesse Sykes, soon to be a newlywed. Jesse had proposed to Charlotte the day after Max and Heather's wedding.

That gave him a perfect diversion: "So when's the wedding?"

"Oh, no you don't. I already told you all about that." It was true. As they'd started cleaning the truck, Jesse had launched into a detailed, play-by-play account of the proposal and Charlotte's "yes." Of course, that only made things worse for Dylan. "This conversation is about you," his pal countered, "not about me."

"Sykes, even the conversations that aren't about you are about you."

Jesse hopped down off the truck and came around to Dylan's side. His face grew serious—well, as serious as his friend got, which wasn't very. "It blew you away, didn't it? You're totally hooked on her, and it's driving you crazy, isn't it?"

Maybe it would be better to admit it to someone. Dylan was just hoping for someone less drastic than Jesse. "Sort of."

"You say that like it's a bad thing."

Dylan threw up his hands. "Isn't it? She has this whole life planned back in Chicago, this amazing job that starts in a matter of days, and I have everything all set up here. I'm in no mood to do a relationship on a 150-mile commute."

"She's running Karl's like a natural. Her grandfather needs to retire, someday if not now. This is a no-brainer as far as I can see."

Dylan rose up to his full height. "She's already got a job. A prime job that will take her exactly where she wants to go. I will not ask a woman to settle for me. I'm nobody's backup plan, got it?"

Jesse had struck a raw nerve, and he had the good sense to know it and back off. "Hey." His tone changed. "No one wants that for you. Or Karla. You're a catch, always have been. If she doesn't opt for you, then it's her loss, buddy."

Dylan didn't offer a reply, more like a grunt of acknowledgment. Jesse was just being Jesse; the guy had fallen for Charlotte hook, line and sinker, and wanted to see the whole world matched up as happily. The trouble was all with Dylan, and he knew it. It wasn't on Jesse that this morning it felt as if the fireman was the last in a long line of Gordon Falls residents conspiring to send Dylan into another heartbreak.

They worked for a while in tense silence, cleaning and rinsing in the warm afternoon sunshine. Then, as if he'd been trying to hold it in and just couldn't any longer, Jesse came back around to Dylan's side of the truck. "What I can't get," he said, tossing a wet rag to the floor at Dylan's feet, "is why you're not even trying. Karla's worth the effort. Yvonne's never been my favorite person, but if you let what she did keep you from fighting for a chance with Karla, well, then she just went to the top of my most hated list." He grabbed Dylan's shoulder. "Come on—you're better than that."

"Look, we talked about it, okay? We both agree it won't work."

Jesse leaned against the truck. "Oh, I can just imagine how you 'talked about it.' You probably even apologized for kissing her, didn't you?"

Dylan refused to answer that.

"You know what your problem is?"

It didn't matter what answer Dylan gave to a question like that, so he remained silent.

Jesse kept right on, determined to finish his lecture. "Your problem is that you think you're being noble."

That wasn't what Dylan was expecting. "Noble?"

"You've got it in your head that you're putting Karla's goals ahead of yours. The whole noble heroic sacrifice bit. Not getting in the way of her chosen future."

Dylan went back to scrubbing a set of dials. "Thanks for making me sound like a doormat of chivalry. I knew I could count on you."

"It's convenient, as far as emotional excuses go. Feels safer to take yourself out of the game and all."

This was starting to get annoying. "Got me all figured out, do you?" Normally he let Jesse get away with a lot, but the guy was toeing up to a line Dylan didn't want him to cross. He was in no mood for one of his "I have matters of the heart all figured out" speeches. He turned his back to Jesse in the futile hope that Sykes would get the hint.

The ornery fireman simply came around to the other side. "Look, I can't think of anyone who fought harder for a different future than you did when you left Chicago. You kicked and scratched and remade your whole life into exactly what you wanted. I admire that." He ducked his head into Dylan's line of vision even when Dylan looked away. "What I don't admire is how you've decided—how you've let Yvonne decide—that you're second-rate somehow. You've let that woman knock all the fight out of you."

"So I should put it all on the line for a chance with Karla. Pour on the charm and sweet-talk her out of her own life's goals and stage a one-man campaign that Gordon Falls could be the perfect home for her." Dylan picked up the bucket of sudsy water and started walking back to the edge of the garage floor. "Because what have I got to lose? In six months there's *no chance* she'll figure out all she's given up and walk right on out of here. No chance *whatsoever* that if we keep up the Coffee Catch, I'll be the one to personally introduce to her some fancy high-priced tourist fisherman who'll fit perfectly back in Chicago."

Dylan hurled the soapy water out of the bucket, sending it splashing halfway across the driveway. "Come on—you said it yourself. That Jim Shoe guy would have been hitting on her if he were ten years younger. I can't keep her here. I don't want to be the only thing keeping her here. It *won't work*." He glared at Jesse, no longer worried about offending his friend. "And that means this conversation is over."

"Hey, Dylan, come on, it's…"

"Over." He stopped himself just short of shouting.

Jesse pushed out a breath and held up his hands in surrender. "Loud and clear, buddy, loud and clear."

Karl had declared his official return to Karl's.

Karla would have thought her grandfather had come back from the dead, the way the coffee shop erupted in cheers and applause as he walked in the front door Tuesday morning. Dad, Violet and even Dr. Morehouse had all expressed concerns, but Grandpa wasn't hearing any of it. Once Karl Kennedy set his mind to something, he was an immovable force. No, his gait wasn't steady, but he wasn't using a walker, either. In fact, the time it had taken him to haul himself up the few front steps had only added to the anticipation of the encouraging crowd. If he'd faltered, Karla was convinced the townsfolk would have surged forward and carried him in on their shoulders.

Dad threw her a look. It didn't take much to

connect the dots—Karl was launching himself back into the shop as his way of handling the news of her return to Chicago. Dad's look wasn't so much of blame as it was of worried acceptance of an unavoidable consequence. Karl had to know she was leaving, and evidently he felt he had to be back here if she was.

"Welcome back, Karl." Oscar managed a smile for the occasion. "We sure have missed you."

"I missed even you, Oscar." Grandpa turned to look around the room, choking up a bit. "I missed all of you."

The room was packed, but parted like the Red Sea to allow Grandpa a clear path to the corner booth, specially decorated for the occasion. "I do believe," Karl laughed as he eased himself carefully down into the booth, "this might be the first time I've sat here in years."

"You've earned it, Pop." Dad clasped a hand on Grandpa's shoulder as he ceremoniously placed a cup of coffee and a slice of pie on the table.

"Does everyone get coffee and pie?" Grandpa asked, his face flushing.

"Today," Karla answered, pulling a cloth off the chalkboard to reveal a festive, illustrated sign Charlotte Taylor had drawn saying Karl

Day—Free Pie for All! "everybody gets all the coffee and pie they want."

Jesse Sykes turned on the music system he'd brought, filling the air with the '40s swing jazz that was Grandpa's favorite, and the party began.

Maybe this was the way it was supposed to be, Karla thought. She'd prayed hard for Grandpa after he'd announced to the family his intended official return to Karl's Monday night at dinner. Perhaps all the happiness in the room was God's answer to those prayers. It seemed as if everyone was offering to pitch in and help. It was heartwarming to see a man so loved, so tied to such a large group of friends.

Dylan came up beside her, shaking his head and chuckling at some joke someone had just made about Karl's "superman bionic hip." He stared for a moment at the crowd around Grandpa. "I think he's going to be okay."

Karla looked up at him. "I sure hope so. I can't help thinking this is my doing." She swallowed the lump in her throat for the hundredth time since Grandpa's announcement.

"You did what you needed to do, and now Karl is doing what he needs to do—there's no blame in that. He may not be able to see it now, but he'd never want to be what stood between you and Rooster's—you know that."

Karla nodded, thankful that Dylan had found the right words to soothe her guilty conscience. She blinked back a tear. "Thanks, I needed to hear that."

Dylan held her gaze for a moment, and she saw the "one that got away" look in his eyes that had pierced her heart back on the riverfront. If only she had met Dylan even one year ago while he was still back in Chicago, how different things might have been. Only, was that true? If they had met in Chicago, then he would never have launched his charter business, and it was clear Dylan belonged on the river as much as she belonged behind the counter of Rooster's someday. The weight of "what if" pressed against her heart, as sad as it was certain.

"Your grandfather's a rich man, Karla. Rich in all the ways that matter." So much hung unresolved and unsaid in the air between her and Dylan.

Karla slid the last slice from a pie tin and set it on the counter in front of Dylan, a hopeful peace offering. "That sounds like a line straight out of *It's a Wonderful Life*."

"It probably is." Dylan swiped his baseball cap from his head and stuffed it in his back pocket. "Look at that guy. A million friends who all wish him the best. That's the way to go through life, isn't it?"

Did she have a million friends who wished her the best? She had Bebe and others from school, even one or two from her high school days, but nothing like Karl's crowd of supporters. "I hope my customers think as highly of me someday." After all, Karl had built up his following over forty years, and she hadn't even started yet. "If I do it right, Rooster's clientele would be as much its own community as this—with maybe a bit less gossip."

Dylan laughed as he dug into his pie. "That'd be nice."

"Will you come visit me at Perk? Once or twice, maybe, if business brings you to Chicago?" It felt like a hollow offer—there was little reason to think business would ever bring him to Chicago. A trade show, maybe, but then again that was *marketing*, and he'd made his disdain for the city pretty clear.

Dylan stopped his forkful of apple pie midair. "Sure, why not?"

Karla wasn't convinced. It wasn't that he was lying—she thought he meant it at the moment, but she was equally sure he'd somehow never find the chance.

Chapter Fourteen

Karl's first few days back at the coffee shop were bumpy, but they went well enough for Karla's worries to ease. Grandpa had consented to hiring two more servers even if he hadn't come around to the fact that someone other than him needed to be managing the place. "All in good time," Dad said, but Karla could tell the topic concerned him, too.

The anniversary celebration was clipping along nicely, as well. Sixteen different groups had signed up their decorated floats for the parade. Some, like the 4-H club with their "Noah's Ark," proudly announced their designs. Others, like the fire department's flaming cabin she wasn't supposed to know about, kept their entries a secret.

While she'd have never thought it at first, it was a hectic sort of fun being in charge of the event. So many people had come up to her in church this morning with a question or comment. It was as if no one even noticed she didn't live here—she'd been grafted into the community without hesitation even as she was thinking about how to pack up her car to move back to Chicago. The dissonance made for an odd sensation that never seemed to leave the pit of her stomach.

"Don't forget next week's special celebration service to honor the Gordon Falls Volunteer Fire Department," Pastor Allen said. "If you signed up to serve on the setup or cleanup crews, see Jeannie Owens for your assignments after church. The event committee will meet in Room 4 after service as well, and the decorations committee will be—"

The firehouse siren cut him off midsentence as it sent up its distinctive wail, and everything halted except the handful of men who got up and dashed out of the sanctuary.

It was one of the things about Gordon Falls that was burned in her memory: the whole town stilled for a second when the fire alarm went off. You could be just about anywhere, and at the sound, there would always be someone who stood up and left the room. Meetings, church, restaurants, picnics—it was the unspoken rule in Gordon Falls that nothing was ever allowed to get in the way of the volunteer firemen rushing to the station to do their jobs.

Grandpa had a policy that no fireman on the shift ever had to pay for an unfinished meal—even though that meant a hefty sum since he was so close to the firehouse. He always joked that he wanted the firemen on his side if the shop ever caught fire, but Karla had long since guessed that Grandpa just figured it was his way to give back. She'd have to find some way to give back to her community when Rooster's opened, whenever and wherever that was.

Karla said a prayer with the whole congregation—as they always did in such an instance—for the health and safety of the victims and the firefighters. One of those who had risen and left was Dylan. *Keep him safe, Lord,* she prayed as she crossed his attendance off the after-service meeting. Unless this was a false alarm, she'd have to handle this meeting on her own.

No worries—she was up to it. They'd talked about this possibility several times, and things were going smoothly in the event plans. As it was, she and Dylan were right on schedule to stage their "spontaneous handoff" to Grandpa and Violet sometime in the next two days. *Thank You, Father, for giving me a smooth exit from Gordon Falls.* Even Grandpa had seemed to lose that hurt look that constantly poked at her conscience.

Twenty minutes later, Karla checked off another item on her anniversary committee agenda. "Okay, so the prizes for best float are all set, right?"

"We could use a few more items in the grand prize, but I'll take care of that," Violet pronounced. Karla and Dylan had joked more than once that Violet Sharpton was their secret weapon. That woman could get anything out of anybody.

"The hall decorations have all been approved, and I'm renting the tables for the outside banquet in front of the firehouse. It'll be like George's retirement party, only about twice the size, so we'll need to block off the street." Abby Reed and Jeannie Owens made an outstanding team heading up that part of the evening. "Only we'll need..."

The door pushed open behind the pair to reveal a rumpled, slightly sweaty Dylan still in his fire gear. "What'd I miss?"

Karla was completely unprepared for the way Dylan looked right off a call. His face was flushed, his T-shirt damp and clinging to a very muscular chest. For a slightly sooty, rough-hewn guy, he looked downright heroic. And from the stares of the other women in the room—including Violet—he was having the same effect on everyone.

"What?" he said, pulling a red suspender down off one shoulder. "I figured if I changed I'd miss the whole meeting. It was just a grass fire—I'm not too messed up." As the women still stared, he added, "Am I?"

"No, hon, you're just fine." Violet smirked. "Sit down and I'll get you a glass of water or something."

"We were almost finished, actually." Karla had to concentrate on spitting the words out. Really, it was ridiculous the way his appearance affected her—it was as if a blinding flashbulb had just gone off in the back of her brain. The unassuming nature she'd always seen in him was gone, as if he put on an air of authority when he donned his gear. She was ashamed of the gush of attraction that muddled her thoughts.

"Here, you can catch up from my notes while Mayor Boston goes over the volunteer sign-ups." She pushed her agenda notes to the empty chair beside her, trying not to think about the woodsy, smoky smell that filled the room as he sat down. She'd have thought a just-off-the-job firemen would not smell as good as he did. There was a smudge of something black on his jaw and the urge to reach out and wipe it off was as strong as it was insane. *Stop that,* she reprimanded herself. *You're being silly.*

"Sounds like plans for the service are all in place. Pastor Allen…?" Karla shoved her thoughts back onto the meeting's agenda.

"Well," the pastor answered, "we thought we'd add a bit where we could light candles for all those who served in the department but are no longer with us."

"We've lost men in the line of duty?" Mayor Boston asked.

"The department has only lost one man on duty—back in the sixties," Chief Bradens replied. "But I pulled the figures for Pastor Allen and there are 172 firefighters to remember over the department's history.

"Then after the service, we can release balloons for all the living firemen and those still serving. You know, let their spouse or children do the honors as a way of recognizing the family commitment."

"I think that's a great idea," Violet said, looking at Chief Bradens and at Dylan. "We can't say enough thank-yous to our heroes."

Later, as the meeting broke up, Karla saw Dylan catch up to Violet in the hallway. "You say thank you to us all the time, Vi. I just want you to know that. You've been great to the firehouse." He towered over the petite woman, and Karla got the sense that if she could reach, Vi would have tousled Dylan's hair or made some other grandmotherly gesture.

"I'm glad you feel that way. We'll be lighting one of those candles for Mr. Sharpton, you know. He was one of you in his younger years."

"You don't say." Dylan's smile spread all the way to his eyes.

Vi poked him in the ribs. "And who's going to hold your balloon, son?"

Karla winced. Violet could be as stubborn as Grandpa, if not more. She edged toward the two of them, ready to step in and divert the conversation if Dylan needed saving.

"Oh, don't you worry about that. I'll find someone to hold my balloon."

Karla thought that was a pretty effective dodge, until the older woman looked straight at her. "I've no doubt that you will, Dylan." With a wink and a chuckle, she headed off to where Grandpa was debating some topic with Mayor Boston.

The color in Dylan's cheeks heightened, and Karla felt her own cheeks burn. She knew they were both trying hard to disregard the gentle hum that had passed between them. The one that had only doubled when they'd mutually decided nothing could be done about it. That was bad enough, but when he did things like show up looking all scruffy and heroic, or treat Violet's outrageous remarks with such tenderness, it just made it all worse.

"I was thinking—" she resorted to event business to cover the discomfort of the moment "—we should ask those two to judge the parade. I don't think either of them is planning on being involved in decorating a boat."

Dylan pretended to look shocked. "Karl's isn't going to enter a sloop dressed as a slice of pie?"

"Very funny. Luckily, this is one instance where Grandpa isn't showing his tendency to stick his nose in every town project. Have you thought about how we're going to pass the leadership off to them?"

Dylan's expression sobered. "I was waiting for you to tell him you were really leaving." He gently touched her elbow. "I'm sorry that was so hard, by the way. But he seems to be holding up okay. Maybe it was the thing he needed to push himself back to the shop."

"Grandpa? He needed no encouragement to come back. We were all struggling to keep him away a bit longer."

"Yeah." Dylan gazed down at her. "But it looks like it worked out."

She dared to bring up the thought that had been niggling at the back of her mind. "Do you still think it's a good idea to foist it all off on Grandpa and Vi? They'll feel responsible for everything, and I'm worried it will stress them out. Won't they have more fun if we simply name them as the boat parade judges?"

"But you're leaving." Why did he have to say it like that? With just enough of a hint of disappointment to send her imagination running amok?

"I know, but I can put it off until Sunday afternoon. Things are going so smoothly that if you can pull most of the weight this final week, I can still be ready to head to Chicago at the last minute. Only I don't want to ask so much of you." She couldn't help but add, "I know we groaned about being stuck with it at first, but, well, I've had fun."

"It has been fun. I'm glad we did it."

She was, too, only her enjoyment of their partnership made everything so much more complicated.

She'd had fun. That was the last thing Dylan wanted to hear.

It was easier when she appeared bored, looked stuck with the small-town celebration that was getting in the way of her big plans.

When she acted as if clocking time in Gordon Falls was just an obligation to her grandfather. That kind of attitude made it easier to write off Karla Kennedy as just another woman on the fast track to her own success. It made it easier to ignore the hum under his rib cage when she gave him one of her looks or pushed to get her way at the coffee shop or around the committee table.

Helping her leave was the right thing to do. They wanted different things from life. Sure, it had felt good to facilitate the connection between her and Jim Shoe, to show her that all the good business in the world didn't stop outside Chicago's borders. She was leaving, should be leaving, and he most definitely was set to stay here in Gordon Falls. So why did her words about leaving burn in his chest the way they did?

"Yeah," he managed, fiddling with a snap on his suspenders, "it has been a pretty good time, despite what we first thought." He didn't want to hand this off to Karl and Violet either, but he wasn't sure it was wise to agree with her new plan. It was getting harder to keep working with her the way his feelings were stubbornly growing. And quite frankly, it wasn't a terribly good idea to be focusing on something other than the charter business right now in the height of the summer. The weather report looked ominous for the next few days, and he hated the thought of charter trips getting postponed or canceled.

Karla shifted her weight, fidgeting. "Well—" she tucked her hair behind her ears "—I just want you to know that I'm okay with seeing this through to the end, despite what we said earlier. Only I feel like it will put a lot on you this week, and I'm not sure that's fair."

It wasn't fair, which couldn't explain why he was so in favor of the idea. "I can handle it. They'll probably have to fuss with my boat from Thursday on anyway, so maybe I'll have extra time on my hands. Especially if the weather's bad."

That drew a frown from her. "Bad weather? There's a forecast for storms this coming weekend?"

She really was invested in this whole thing. "They're calling for some good-sized rainstorms Wednesday and Thursday night."

Now she looked alarmed. "Won't rain ruin everything?"

City girl. "Folks out here are used to the weather, Karla. As long as it stays dry enough Saturday night, we'll be fine. It might even raise the river a little bit, which will only give us a good current for the parade."

"If everyone's got their float stored inside."

He could only laugh. "Boats float on water. They'll be on water in the parade. No one's going to make boat parade decorations that can't withstand a little water."

"Well, as long as it's just a little water. I'm not going to stand on the riverbank in a downpour to watch this parade."

Chapter Fifteen

The downpour had started Tuesday night and hadn't let up yet. The "bit of bad weather" had turned into a full-fledged major storm. The only piece of good news was that it was currently projected to clear out by Friday, but that didn't help the charter trip Dylan had booked for this morning. With the parade commandeering the *High Tide* starting on Thursday night, this rain had just washed out his only booking for the week.

He couldn't blame the customers for calling and canceling last night when the rain set in. Who wanted to fish in a downpour? Still, the nonrefundable deposit wasn't anything close to the full price of a charter trip for eight, and the difference made a dent in this month's income. The Coffee Catches had helped a lot, but that didn't mean he was yet in a position to comfortably endure a stretch of bad weather.

Sighing, Dylan closed the lid on his laptop showing the weather report. He'd checked it four times since 5:00 a.m., and things were only growing worse. The rain was near roaring against his kitchen window, slashing down in steep angles that spoke of high winds. It was time to lash down the boat and hope for the best. Happy to own a set of professional-grade rain gear, Dylan took a deep breath as he did up the final snap before pulling the door open and heading out into the storm.

The lights were on at Karl's as he drove by. It didn't surprise him, despite the foul weather. The coffee shop was always the place to ride out a storm. It had become a Gordon Falls tradition—Karl's stayed open in any storm. They were on somewhat high ground, had a generator if power went out and company was always a good defense against threatening weather.

Was Karla ready for the challenge of keeping Karl's open in a storm? Was Karl? Could the old man even make it in? Karla lived right above the shop so she'd be there for sure, but this seemed too much for the old man to take on at this point in his recovery. He tried to peer into the shop windows to see her, but as it was, Dylan was hard-pressed to see even three feet ahead of his own headlights. The pooled water on many of the side streets told him what his laptop weather report had already proclaimed: the river was rising.

Dylan wasn't the only person preparing their boats for the storm. "Nasty stuff!" called Yorky, who owned a boat on the dock next to the *High Tide.* Yorky's boat was much smaller than his—a pleasure craft rather than Dylan's charter boat—but size wasn't an advantage in weather like this. "She gonna be okay?" Yorky, like almost every other boater Dylan had ever known, referred to all watercraft as females. Only tourists called a boat an "it."

"Well," he yelled back, wiping the water from his eyes in what felt like a futile gesture, "this is turning out to be a big one, but I think we'll ride it out fine." The truth was, today's weather was looking as if it might be the largest storm Dylan had seen since purchasing the *High Tide.* He was starting to feel a nagging doubt in the pit of his stomach that the weekend's celebrations might very well be in danger.

Dylan pushed aside that worrisome thought as Yorky came over and held out his hand for the other end of the rope Dylan was holding.

"This river gets angry when she overflows. There's too much coming down off the ridge. Summer's been too dry to handle it."

"I know." Dylan made an extra knot in the line as he moved the mooring from its normal position on the floating dock to high up on the piling that held the dock in place. His cell phone had begun to spout flash flood warnings on the drive over here.

"If she breaks free," Yorky warned, "you'll find her fifty miles downriver. Maybe in splinters."

"She'll be okay." There was more certainty in Dylan's voice than in his gut. "Thanks for the concern." He began taking down the canopy and anything else that would allow the wind to knock the boat around. "At least she'll fare better than those sailboats over there." On the other bank of the river sat a half dozen sailboats with no one seeing to their security. That was a problem; if one of those broke free—which was likely if no one was preparing them for the storm—they wouldn't necessarily head straight downriver as Yorky predicted. They could just as easily drift across the river and do serious damage to the *High Tide* and her dockside neighbors.

"Weekenders," Yorky growled, following

Dylan's line of thinking. "Well, it's not like we can take 'er out to sea where she'd be safer."

It was true; even though it didn't make much sense at first, a boat out at sea was always safer than one tied to something fixed like a dock. "No ocean handy in Illinois, Yorky. We'll just have to make do with what we've got." The wind whipped rain in his face as he began to empty the *High Tide* of its contents, tossing all the cushions and large items into a locker bolted to the dock. The smaller stuff—tackle boxes, rods and reels, coolers, and even all the movable electronic equipment—went into a rolling locker that he would put in his truck.

Keep her safe, Lord, Dylan prayed as he worked to secure the boat he'd come to love. *High Tide* meant so much to him; a chance to start life over, the opportunity to be his own man. He wasn't at all sure he had it in him to start over a third time if the boat was demolished.

Still, it wasn't as if he didn't know this was a possibility. Storms large and small were part of life on the river. God's creation was beautiful and peaceful and majestic, but it could also choose to flex a muscle or two and show an awesome power. Any fisherman who lost a healthy, fearful respect for the water soon learned what a brutal foe a river could be.

As the storm picked up strength, Dylan and Yorky stopped trying to talk as they pulled the extra buoys from the dock—useful in normal weather but dangerous in a storm. Dylan found himself in an active state of prayer, asking God for the safety of his boat, his friends, the guys at the firehouse, the owners of the other boats on the dock and Karla.

Every once in a while he would straighten up and look west, hoping to spy a wedge of brighter sky. Instead, it seemed the sky only grew darker. Even if the *High Tide* rode out the storm intact, Dylan had already lost. Like a farmer, he depended upon forces beyond his control; fish, weather and the fickle nature of the river. When it was good, it was glorious. But when it was bad, it was a disaster. Today, the whole balance played out right before his eyes on a grander scale.

"Well, at least they're bow into the wind." Yorky had spoken what Dylan had just thought; it was by God's grace that both his and Yorky's boats were docked facing into the wind—the position where they were safest. For now.

"We've done all we can." He wanted the

statement to give him courage, but instead it seemed to feed the feeling of helplessness.

"Time to go inside and wait it out. Godspeed, son. I hope we're laughing about this on Friday." With a wave, Yorky set off to his own car, and Dylan hoisted the locker into the payload of his truck.

The miserable feeling only compounded as he drove back to his apartment. Every part of him was wet, cold and muddy. His muscles ached and he'd cut himself in several places. Even swiping at top speed, his windshield wipers could barely carve out a wedge on the glass long enough for him to see. Thunder rumbled regularly across the sky, and the air smelled of storm, the tang of lightning's ozone setting his nerves on edge.

Once inside, he shed his sopping clothes and pulled a dry T-shirt over his head. With every motion, he fought the urge to head to Karl's. There was no true reason to head back out into the storm and over there. After all, he could just as easily check in on Karla and the shop by phone. If he knew Karl, the old man would be worried sick back at his house, unable to stand at his time-honored post, keeping Karl's a safe open haven in any storm. He could understand the frustration; for him it would be like being lashed to a tree while forced to watch a house burn. To know what you ought to be doing and not be able to do it? That was one of life's cruelest tortures.

It was why—or part of why—he couldn't bring himself to be the thing standing between Karla and Rooster's.

His resistance lasted all of ten minutes. By the time he'd put on dry pants, threw down a second mediocre cup of coffee—which only stoked the urge to brave a downpour to get to Karl's—he was pacing his living room, stuffing his hands in his pants pockets to keep from reaching for his cell phone.

It's closer to the firehouse, he told himself as he reached again for rain gear. *I'm not on duty, but if they call I can be there in a flash.* Of course, that line of thinking also meant that anyone from the firehouse was already close enough to help Karla should she need assistance, but Dylan chose to deny that fact. The fact he couldn't ignore was the steady inner insistence that if anyone was going to help Karla ride out the storm and keep Karl's open, it was going to be him.

"I know, Grandpa." Karla tried to keep the frustration out of her voice. Her grandfather had called four times in the past hour. "I'm downstairs and we're open. Oscar's here, and there are a bunch of others here, too. I agree with Dad—you need to stay put."

"You know what to do? You know where the generator is?" Grandpa's voice pitched up with every new question. Part of her wanted to remind him that it was hard to stay open if she was spending all of her time answering the phone, but another part of her was grateful for Grandpa's voice. The burden of keeping Karl's open in a storm was starting to press down harder than she liked.

"I saw it in the back utility closet." She wasn't exactly sure how to work it, but appliances came with directions, and Grandpa was sure to call again. "We're okay. So far so good, as far as the power goes." *Please, Lord, could You keep it that way?*

"Keep the coffee going and feed anyone who comes in the door. Karl's stays open in a storm." It must have been the tenth time Grandpa had given her that order.

"I know. And I should go do that, okay? My cell phone's cutting in and out, but the landline to the shop still works fine so call there next time." There would be a next time, and she was rather glad of that. For the first time since she'd arrived in Gordon Falls, Karla felt too young to be holding up a business all on her own. Which was funny, considering she'd spent the past three years planning to do just that.

"Take care of the shop for me." Karla hated the desperation in her grandfather's voice. "Is Vi there yet? She should be there by now."

"I'm sure she's on her way, Grandpa." The thought of those two together, looking out for each other, struck a warm glow in her heart. They were so good for each other; anyone could see that. Grandpa deserved to be happy. And he also deserved to know his shop was in good hands. "I've got to go take care of business now. Kennedys can do, right? And Karl's stays open in a storm."

"That it does, girlie, that it does."

Karla liked the brightness that returned to her grandfather's voice, and she let it bolster her spirits until she checked the weather notifications on her smartphone. The radar screen showed a menacing train of powerful storms lined up one after the other. A red bar ran across the top with the ominous words, *Flood Warning for the entire Gordon River floodplain.*

Flood? A power outage was one thing, but keeping Karl's open during a flood? That felt like a whole different level of disaster. Mom was at home twenty miles away where she was safe, Dad was with Grandpa—which is where he belonged—and the floodgates were there to keep floods from getting downtown, right?

Karla tightened the knot around her apron, grabbed another bag of coffee grounds from the stock shelf and headed out to where the customers were. *Kennedys can do. Just keep saying that to yourself. Kennedys can do.*

And what Kennedys can't do, God can.

Chapter Sixteen

By the time he made the ten-minute trek to Karl's, Dylan might have walked into the GFVFD shower stall. He was soaked again, chilly from the whipping wind and already feeling tired. All he wanted was to know Karla was getting along fine, and to spend ten minutes sipping one of her steaming hot cups of coffee. The wind was driving the rain so hard it took a large amount of effort to pull the shop's front door open.

Still, he was instantly glad he came. As if to endorse his choice, the lights gave an ominous flicker as he shut the door and stood dripping onto Karl's welcome mat.

Karla looked brave but bedraggled, standing over a bucket in the middle of the room and staring up at a leak in the expanse of the ceiling that stretched beyond the shelter of the upstairs apartment. Surrounding her was the handful of customers he knew would be in the shop riding out the nasty weather. She looked desperately glad to see him, the relieved look in her eyes settling way down in his chest. He knew, in that moment, that he would have swum here if it came to that.

"Hi." Her voice had an "I'm putting on my brave face" tightness to it that made his heart pinch.

"How's everything holding up?" He was almost afraid to ask her in front of everyone, but the people in the shop now were more like family than customers.

"You know Karl's," she said, shrugging as she looked up at the dripping ceiling. "We're always open in a storm."

"It's a Karl's tradition," he said. He noticed the empty bucket beside the counter and picked it up, swapping it out from under the drip for her and walking with the full one toward the sink.

"I remember riding out a few storms with Grandpa at the shop when I was younger. Somehow it seemed a lot more fun back then."

"I suspect it's a lot more fun to ride out a storm in Karl's than to be the one making sure Karl's rides out the storm." He tipped the bucket into the sink. "Your grandfather okay?"

"He calls about every fifteen minutes." She eyed him. "You're soaked."

"Not too bad." He didn't want her worrying about him right now. "Just in need of hot coffee."

"That, I can offer." She reached for the carafe he knew held her special, stronger brew. He liked that he had access to Karla's personal blend. "One sugar, no cream." He liked even more that she knew just how he took his coffee.

One sip of the stuff sent warmth out to his fingertips. "Best cup in the county. Did you stay dry?"

"Mostly." He watched her shoulders ease up a bit, and enjoyed the possibility that his mere presence helped ease her tension. "My commute is just down a flight of stairs."

"I know Karl is glad of that. You can't stay open in a storm if you can't get here." He tried to make the tradition sound like an adventure rather than a burden.

"Oh, he tried to make Dad bring him in, but no one is letting him out in this. I told Emily to stay home, too." A blast of thunder rattled the front windows, and they both turned around. "Wow," she said quietly, "look at it out there."

"This is going to be a big one," Oscar

warned from his seat at the counter. "I'd better head to the store. We're liable to lose power soon." As if they'd heard him, the lights flickered again. The old man drained his coffee and set his face in grim determination. "I'll get soaked."

"Oscar, are you sure? You really will get soaked, and I don't think you'll have any customers today." Dylan felt his wet shirt sticking to his back. At least it was warmer in here and he knew Karla was holding up okay so far.

The lights flickered two more times, causing everyone in the room to look up and groan in distress. Dylan heard a sound from the back of the shop, and turned at the same moment Karla did to see a dark puddle creeping from under the store shelves. "There's water coming in the back door."

They both darted to the back of the shop, where a quick peek out the door revealed a steady stream of water sloughing off the slanted alley that backed up to Karl's rear entrance. It wasn't raised so that delivery dollies could roll up to the door. "That small drain can't keep up with all that water," Karla moaned.

"Not for long," Dylan agreed. He found a broom, and then reopened the door to sweep away the mound of debris piling up around the drain. It helped a little, but not enough, and he got rather wet in the process.

"I'll get some dish towels, and we can pile them up against the door," Karla said. It was a good idea, but it probably wouldn't hold for long. If it kept raining, the runoff from the hillside above Tyler Street would just grow stronger.

Once they'd secured the back door, he followed Karla back into the front of the coffee shop. Although it was nearly 9:00 a.m., the sky was as dark as twilight. The streetlamps were on up and down the avenue, but even they had begun to flicker ominously as the power cut in and out. The worst of the storm was bearing down upon them.

Karla did not like the look on the policeman's face as he shook off his wet coat after walking in the front door. "The river's rising fast." She flinched every time the lights blinked. Nerves were beginning to string tight amongst the customers, and it didn't look as if the rain was letting up anytime soon. "She's up two feet and she's not done yet."

She wiped the last of the water off her hands with her apron. "Is two feet a lot?"

"Not yet, but the forecast said ten inches of rain," Dylan said as he pointed to the television. The map on the screen seemed consumed by dire red patches indicating "extreme" rainfall. Her cell phone had warned the same thing, but she didn't need any technology to tell her this was no small storm; the roar from the rain hitting the windows hadn't let up in hours.

The police officer sighed wearily as she set a cup of coffee down in front of him. "Road closures are starting."

She found his tone entirely too calm. It wasn't as if Karla was going to leave anytime soon, but somehow the knowledge that she might not *be able to leave* tightened the knot already growing in her stomach. She had to be in Chicago by Sunday night. Her brain told her that was still possible, but her stomach seemed eager to start panicking right now.

A glance at the television showed a crawler across the bottom of the screen advising "relocation to higher ground." She looked at Dylan. "Are we 'higher ground'?"

She did not like that he chose his answer carefully. "Depends."

Karla looked out the window. "On what?" The river had crept onto the grassy banks, and pylons of the footbridge that could normally be seen were underwater. No question, the water was creeping toward the levee, but that's what the levee was for—to stop the rising water.

"Are we higher than the river? Yes. Are we high enough not to flood? Well, that depends on the flood."

One of the customers ended a cell-phone call. "The underpass is flooded."

To her relief, the customer didn't sound wildly alarmed. Underpasses in Chicago flooded all the time. "When do they close the floodgates? I mean, that's what they're for, right?"

Another customer piped up as Violet came through the front door. "Closed 'em a few years ago. Got eight feet then. Nasty stuff."

"So now you get to find out what it's like to keep Karl's open in a storm," the older woman said as she leaned her umbrella against the wall. Violet looked entirely too tiny to be out in anything like this. "Not the kind of good-bye you were looking for from the Gordon River, but it sure is exciting." She came over and gave Karla a soggy hug.

"Have you ever seen them close the floodgates, Vi?"

"Like Rudy said, they closed 'em back in '96 when the river rose eight feet. My front door was underwater." She shrugged. "It's what rivers do—rise."

Karla tried not to reason that eight feet was taller than anyone currently in the room. The floodgates were something like twenty feet high and looked reassuringly strong. Grandpa had told her stories of downtown business clipping right along with a flood raging behind those floodgates. People came downtown to watch the floodgates in action, as if it were a spectacle instead of a safety precaution. No reason to worry, right? Still, a loud thunderbolt shook the glasses on the shelving behind her as if to say "don't be so sure."

"I'm going to check in on Dad and Grandpa."

Karla ducked back into the soggy office alcove and made the call on her cell. Everything was okay at the house, but she didn't like that the call dropped twice in the space of four minutes. She also didn't welcome the thought of Dad and Grandpa unable to call for help, or her having to hold down Karl's without being able to call for advice or instructions. Still, she had the landline. Those didn't cut out, right?

Dylan came into the back and poked at the makeshift dam of dish towels. "Everything okay?"

"For now." She pushed up her sleeves. "Karl's stays open in a storm. I've known that my whole life. The promise just feels a bit harder now that I'm the one who has to make it happen."

"If something happens, we can shuttle them over to the firehouse, but I don't think that will be necessary. Karl's is safe."

She was surprised it hadn't occurred to her before. "What about your boats? The river is rising—are they safe?" She'd become surprisingly attached to those boats, for she had such wonderful memories of her time in them.

He scratched his chin, tawny stubble revealing he hadn't yet shaved this morning. "I went out and tied the big boat down special an hour ago. The little one is already on land—I pulled her out to do a little maintenance over the weekend."

"So they'll be okay?" Dylan's whole life was tied up in those boats—he'd mourn their damage the same way Grandpa would grieve anything happening to Karl's.

"For now." She didn't like the way his jaw worked when he said that. Just as she didn't like the way he was staring at the shop's back door.

"If you need to go check on them, go. I'll be okay."

"Thanks, but there isn't much I can do right now. Let's get back up front so we can take care of the customers."

Did he realize he'd said "we"? She did. The long morning ahead seemed a little easier with Captain McDonald by her side.

Chapter Seventeen

Walking back out into the front of the shop, Dylan felt the air of camaraderie that seemed to help combat everyone's tensions. Karl knew what he was doing when he promised to stay open in town emergencies and storms. People needed a place to know they weren't alone.

"Did I ever tell you Yorky's story of how people actually slept in Karl's for two days during a snowstorm once? He said that…" The lights flickered again. All talk halted. Then, in the quiet pause that followed, they gave out and the room fell into the dim blue-green glow of a stormy morning.

Even though it made no sense, Dylan could hear Karla hold her breath. He could feel her hopeful prayer as if she'd spoken the words aloud. For a brief second the light returned, eliciting a cry of relief from Karla and all the gathered customers. Mere seconds later they cut out again, and even Karla seemed to realize what he knew—this time they were out for good.

She looked around, her face cast in pale shadow as she slowly set down the coffee carafe she'd been holding. Surely Karl had told her what to do in a power outage, hadn't he? She looked a little panicked.

"Did Karl show you how to run his generator? He must have one for the fridge and stuff."

That snapped her to action. "Yes. Back here." She started to head for the kitchen behind the counter, but then stopped and turned to face the room. "You all can stay here for as long as you need. Coffee's on the house for as long as it stays warm. Don't go out into this if you don't have to."

At that moment, she sounded so much like her grandfather that Dylan felt his heart twist. She was more born to this than even she realized. She was all the best of Karl wrapped up in a small, lovely, just-the-right-amount-of-feisty package.

She called after Oscar as the old man put his hand on the shop's doorknob. "That means you, too, Mr. Halverson. You won't get far in this deluge."

Oscar simply snorted, pulled his hat down farther and plunged out into the storm.

Karla grunted in worry after the man, exactly how her grandfather would have. Dylan touched her elbow in reassurance. "He'll be okay. He's got food to look after in an outage, too, and he's lived here his whole life." He couldn't help but add, "It's sweet of you to worry. About all of them." He hoped she took that for the compliment that it was. "You were showing me where the generator is?"

She led him back to the storage room and opened a utility closet. He was glad to see a large, sturdy generator—Karl was a sensible guy. "Gas?" he asked, starting to wheel the big contraption out toward the back docks.

"He said there's a full gas tank out on the dock. I'm just supposed to fill it and start her up." She bit her lip and pushed the hair out of her eyes. "However you do that."

She'd never done it, and had no idea how. He knew generators had to be run outside, which meant that unless he was going to stand there and watch Karla figure it out—which of course, he absolutely would not—he was about to get wet. Wett*er*. Oh, well. Before she could put up one syllable of an argument, he pushed open the door and headed out into the downpour.

Five sopping minutes later, Dylan shouted, "Take this in toward the freezer," through the back door, shaking the rain from his eyes while he shielded the power cord from the worst of the torrent. Lightning cracked overhead and Dylan turned to watch the rain running in sheets down the alley toward Tyler Street. With one last check of the generator, he tucked the can of gasoline close to the shop and out of the rain and pulled open the door to come inside. More water gushed onto the storage room floor, and the wind sent papers and box lids tumbling everywhere. Grunting, he tucked the power cord under the weather stripping and shoved the door shut. Relative quiet greeted him as he stood dripping onto the floor. Karla stood up from plugging the chest freezer into the power cord, a look of pity on her face.

"You're soaked."

She was wet herself, her shirt splattered dark with rain and hair sticking to her cheeks in gentle arcs. It wasn't as if he could deny his present state. "Um, yeah." He fought the urge to shake like a dog. "But you've at least got power for now. It doesn't come right back on out here like you may be used to in the city, though."

When another big crack of thunder announced the strengthening storm, she jumped.

She was trying very hard to hide her fear, but he could see right through the bravado. "Not a fan of storms, huh?"

"Not like this."

"Part of life on the river."

Karla found a dish towel and handed it to him. "Are you sure your boats will be okay?"

What he needed was a complete change of clothes—not a two-foot swath of cotton—but at least he could dry his face and hands. "I think so. Water and boats tend to get along." He pulled his now-cold T-shirt away from his skin. "Better than me."

"You're really soaked." She began rummaging through boxes behind Karl's desk. "We've got to at least have a shirt in here somewhere, maybe in the lost and found." After a second, she produced an old and rather small T-shirt. "You won't make any fashion statements, but at least you'll be warm and dry."

Dylan wasn't in any position to argue fashion. He peeled his soaked shirt off over his head and reached for the one she offered.

All scraggly wet hair and rain-soaked arms, Dylan was incredibly attractive. Karla had always heard comments about how fit firemen had to be, but up close…well, stunning didn't quite cover it. He seemed unaware of how close he was to her, how droplets landed on her face as he rubbed the towel over his hair.

"Thank you," she choked out, realizing he'd soaked himself on her behalf. She knew he probably had a thousand things to do right now—either for the department or his boats—but he'd chosen to come and see if she was okay. Practically, she was glad for that; she'd never fueled and started a generator before, and she'd likely have been swimming by the time she'd have managed to work it.

It was more than practicality, though. Far more. It was that tug, that pull between them that had started long before the tango. That unforgettable dance had only forced them to admit it. She had thought that getting it out in the open would defuse it.

Only it hadn't. It had done the opposite— made her aware of him whenever he was near. It made her notice how the tone of his words warmed when he spoke to her. It focused her senses on how he paid attention to others, how he looked straight at people when he spoke to them. There was something uniquely, compellingly authentic about Dylan McDonald. What she had first put down to a lack of drive turned out to be a gift for being "in the moment" with people and situations.

She knew plenty of people whose attention was always just the slightest bit divided between herself and the next conversation, the person behind her, the next task on their list. Dylan was always right where he was—paying attention and displaying a rare contentment that wasn't the opposite of ambition but rather the ultimate display of purpose. A purpose that was, at this moment, fully trained on helping her.

"Really, thanks," she repeated, flustered by the realizations flooding her brain to distraction.

He pulled the towel off his head, his eyes bright and his hair sticking out in all directions. "Least I could do." His words were calm and unassuming, as if service and assistance came to him naturally, like breathing.

Like the breaths that were currently escaping her. Who could take a deep breath with a handsome, dripping wet, grinning firefighter staring at you like that? After having done something so heroic—without even being asked? Really, any woman would have to have lost her pulse not to feel the buzz tingling through her chest at the moment.

She must have gasped or something, because it seemed to dawn on him at that moment how very close they were standing. And the fact that the tight fit of the too-small T-shirt only served to highlight his muscular physique. She'd always thought him handsome, but standing there he was downright jaw-dropping. Karla swallowed hard and pushed the hair out of her eyes with the back of her hand. "We'll have to bring one of the coffee machines back here or we'll run out of coffee up front."

He smiled at her. "Karl's has to stay open."

"And it will, thanks to you."

"I want to help." He said it as if it meant so much more than keeping the power on. The words wrapped around her with a force she wasn't expecting. "A flood's nothing to take casually."

"So it really is a flood?" she squeaked out. A power outage was one thing, but she wasn't nearly ready to deal with anything that sounded so catastrophic. Now she found herself slightly panicked that he might be called away and leave her to deal with this on her own.

Dylan touched her elbow, and Karla felt a spark as if the generator had just surged in her fingertips. "Hey," he said reassuringly, "it'll be fine."

"I don't know what to do in a flood." When had the mantle of Karl's settled so fiercely on her shoulders? When had she started to care so deeply that she found the threat of tears tightening her throat?

He tipped her chin up, the touch sending a second wave of electricity through her. "Hey," he said with enormous warmth in his eyes, "it's not just you. I'm here. And you're the future owner of the fabulous Rooster's, remember? You've got this." Another bolt of thunder shook the building, a few yelps of alarm coming from the front of the shop. "We'd better go calm them down."

Calm me down, Karla thought, caught off guard by the surge of attraction to this man. She nodded toward the large refrigerator no longer humming behind them. *When in doubt, feed people.* "Grab whatever looks like good breakfast food out of there and meet me out front. Breakfast is on the house." As she headed out, another thought struck her. "What about the guys across the street? Do the firemen need to eat?"

"I suspect they'll end up out on call soon enough, but I'll call them anyway." He smiled. "That's nice of you."

She put off the tingle in her chest with a

forced laugh. "Hey, I might need them to save me in an hour or so."

Karla walked back into the front of the store to find a dozen more people shucking off coats and murmuring about the storm. The words "big flood" poked up through the buzz of conversation far too often for her liking.

Violet put down her cell phone. "The church basement has started seeping water over there and at the library, too. The road to Karl's house will probably be underwater soon."

Karla realized she hadn't received a call from Grandpa in over twenty minutes. "Oh, no. Have you tried calling over there?"

"Service is out. Landlines went down about ten minutes ago."

It wasn't as if they were cut off from civilization—or even from cell service, but Karla felt her pulse go up a notch as she passed out towels to the other doused residents who stood dripping on the floor. Things were steadily getting worse. "I'll try to get Dad on his cell right now, okay?"

Dylan appeared, arms full of bread, eggs, cheese, sausage and a few other things. "Karla said breakfast is on the house this morning folks. Everyone pitch in and we'll do just fine."

Violet winked at Karla. "You've got more of

Karl in you than you know. It's exactly what your grandfather would have done."

A month ago, those words would have sat uncomfortably on Karla's spirit. Right now, however, they rushed warm and welcoming through her veins. She looked at all these bedraggled people—so many of whom had become friends over the past weeks—and felt the urge to take care of them. She *did* have this. She did know what to do.

A minute later, she got through to her father's cell phone as she stood near the back of the shop. "Dad? Everything okay over there?"

He sounded tired. "The water's coming up the drive, but we're holding our own. You all right?"

"Power's out, but you can tell Grandpa the generator's up and running and we're making breakfast for everyone who's here. Vi's here, and Oscar was here but he was too worried about the store not to go check on it." At that moment Dylan walked up to where she was standing, holding out a doughnut and a cup of coffee in an amusing role reversal of their first meeting. *My hero,* a grateful little voice in her head declared, and she smiled as she spoke into the phone. "Dylan helped me with the generator." She felt a small swell in her chest as she added, "So yeah, we're actually doing all right."

"Is that Karla? Is she okay?" Grandpa shouted into the phone from what sounded like the kitchen.

"She's doing just fine, Dad," her father called, his voice turned away from the receiver. "Feeding the customers and she's got the generator running."

"That's my girl!" Grandpa exclaimed. "Karl's stays open in any storm. Watch the back hallway—it leaks."

He'd said it so loud even Dylan heard it. He nodded, grabbed a nearby bucket, and set off to play hero again at the back towel dam. How grateful she was to have him here.

"There's a big flood coming," Dad said, soft enough that Karla guessed he was trying to hide the fact from Grandpa. "I'm glad you mother's safe at home. I will get Grandpa ready to evacuate, but let's hope it doesn't come to that."

Karla didn't like the sound of that. "If you might have to evacuate, wouldn't it be better to just leave now?"

"Not yet. Another foot or two, though, and we won't have a choice. It wouldn't be smart to wait until the last minute with the way Grandpa is."

"Don't wait. Come over to the shop now. Dylan says we're on higher ground, right?"

"I don't want to take your grandfather out in this if I can avoid it. If he fell on wet pavement, well, we'd be right back where we started."

Dylan returned, wiping his hands on a towel. He raised his eyebrow in a silent "everything okay?" expression.

Karla shrugged in answer to his query. She couldn't honestly say if everything was okay—it sure didn't feel like it was. "Dad…"

"Why are we sitting here? The shop's on higher ground for crying out loud!"

"Dad, please don't wait. They're saying it will only get worse."

As if God were backing up her point, another loud boom of thunder seemed to shake the whole world. "Okay, I suppose you're right. I'll sandbag the back door and we'll head on in." Karla didn't like the way his words sounded like bracing for battle. "See you in half an hour or so."

Chapter Eighteen

Karla seemed to crumple in on herself, as if all the courage she'd mustered over the past hour had fled at the sound of her father's voice. She looked up at Dylan with the cell phone in her hand, and he felt another little bit of his heart give way.

"They're getting out of Grandpa's house." She swallowed hard. "It's safer here."

"That's good," he said softly, unsure whether touching her would make things better, or simply send her to pieces. She'd been holding up so amazingly well under a terrific strain. "They will be safer here."

In truth, he didn't know that. The street behind the shop had all but become a waterfall, and he'd had to pile up even more towels and plastic bags against the back door. When it came time to refuel the generator—if the machine even stayed running with all that moving water around it—it'd be like tipping a barrel of water down the back hallway. He needed to be here to help, so it was a good thing he wasn't on duty at the firehouse. "Hey, try not to worry. This isn't the first flood in Gordon Falls. People know what to do."

"Yeah." She wrung her hands on the artsy apron she wore.

Keep her busy until Karl and Kurt get here. "Half the shift is heading over to eat breakfast." He put his hand on her back, steering her in the direction of the tables out front. "The other half will swap out in half an hour—unless there's a call."

Together they walked out into the front of the shop, now a collection of people in various levels of soaked and afraid. The communal sense that this was no ordinary storm had begun to permeate the room. "The firefighters will be coming over in a minute," he announced. "Let's get ready to feed them."

It was exactly what Karla needed—she kicked into gear, organizing preparations and setting out dishes. When the ten men came sloshing through the door, Karla had food hot and ready. Karl's was serving as the town hub the way it always had, and Dylan felt a glow of admiration for the little dynamo of a woman at the helm. He knew from experience that feeding ten hungry firemen was no small feat. Even Jesse, the best cook in the firehouse, had offered his compliments for the huge meal Karla set out.

For a while, the room was filled with companionable chatter, the camaraderie of everyone caught in the storm. All that stopped when the signal came. The room quieted instantly. Dylan pushed out a breath and a prayer along with it—things had just officially gone from bad to worse, and Karl and Kurt were still out there.

"What's that?" Karla asked, catching on to the growing unease among the townsfolk. "It can't be a fire… It's not coming from the firehouse, is it?"

Dylan held Karla's gaze as steadily as he could. "That's the signal that they're closing the floodgates."

"Haven't done that in years," Violet said. "That can't be good."

"Can't be good" was an understatement. The floodgates closed off Route 20, the main route in and out of Gordon Falls. Deploying the floodgates meant that the river was projected to rise and keep rising. Dylan had never actually seen it done, but he knew the mechanics and, more importantly, the implications. What was on this side of the floodgates would be saved from the worst of the flood. What was on the outside, however, was another story.

His boats were outside the floodgates. People's homes were outside the floodgates. The highway was outside the floodgates. And while the town wasn't entirely cut off when the gates where shut, access was hampered enough to make a real difference. It took an hour longer to get into town if help had to arrive from the other direction.

"It's a precaution," he said, mostly for Karla's benefit. "It works well. I've seen the photos."

Violet Sharpton caught his eye, silently mouthing "Karl," with a grave look on her face. His house was on the other side of the floodgates.

"I remember back in '72 before the gates," Yorky, who'd lived in Gordon Falls his entire life, said over his plateful of eggs. "The way the water went through town…"

"Hey," Dylan cut him off with a cheerful tone to mask his sharp glare, "not really a good time for those stories, don't you think?"

"Yeah." Yorky was smart enough to catch Dylan's meaning. "Better not to tell that one, huh?"

The siren's wail died down, but the conversation in the shop didn't truly pick up. It was more like a cautious murmuring between the customers. Had Karla figured it out yet? She looked scared, eyes darting around the room, listening hard. He found himself waiting for some huge sound, as if one could hear the great metal boom of the gates shutting from miles away. Dylan had no idea if that was true, but he imagined the sound might make anyone's blood run cold. He sent up another silent prayer that God would protect Gordon Falls, and looked up to notice Violet's and several other heads bowed in what he could only assume was the same.

Karla went very still. "Grandpa's house is on the other side, isn't it?"

He couldn't let her train of thought go there. "But they are on their way here—remember? They'd have gotten to this side of the gates by now, I'm sure of it."

"Grandpa's slow. What if the drive was blocked? Or a tree went down? What if they're not?"

Dylan gripped her shoulders. "It's only a ten-minute drive—I'm sure they made it inside and they'll walk in the door any second. But if by some chance they ran into trouble, remember that your dad and grandfather have lived in Gordon Falls for a long time. They know what to do in a flood. They'll find whatever high ground they can and they'll be okay."

Karla pulled her cell phone from her apron pocket, flipped it open and dialed. From where he stood, Dylan could hear the three-toned signal indicating a dropped call. She tried again as he looked at his own phone, but the storm had impeded service. He could see the fear building in her eyes. "If they're not here soon," he offered, "I'll go look for them."

Keep her busy. Dylan picked up the coffee carafe and handed it to her. "Go do what you do best. They'll be here. Think how proud your grandfather will be to come in and see Karl's up and running in a storm." When she didn't move, he nudged her forward. "Go on."

The door pushed open, a burst of sound and water that snapped every head in the room toward the direction of the door, and a soaking wet Jesse Sykes stood in the entrance. "Second shift, on its way."

With that, the firemen currently in the room hurried to finish their breakfast. The shop was filled with noise again as firefighters piled dishes and said goodbye to the other customers, who wished them well as they went back to the firehouse. Dylan was glad for the burst of activity to keep Karla occupied.

Dylan took Jesse aside. "What's the word?"

His pal lost his usual carefree expression. "Eight feet or higher over the next two hours. I sure am glad Charlotte is up at Chief Bradens's house with Melba and Maria—that house is one of the highest in town."

Eight feet. The floodgates were ten feet. They would hold out the worst of it unless the water surged. And water running over dry ground had a habit of surging. "We'll just pray the gates hold, then."

"Only..." Jesse's expression said everything his words did not.

Dylan felt a chill settle deep into his gut that had nothing to do with wet socks. "Only what?"

The fireman shook his head. "I...well, I can't confirm anything."

"Sykes, what?"

"Chad says he's worried the gate won't actually hold."

Chad Owens was the fire inspector, and as such had many connections to the various town hall departments. He was also known to be a stickler for codes and ordinances—a man in charge of public safety who took his job very seriously. "What do you mean 'not hold'? That can't be true."

"Chad told me they found some rusting

in the hinges and the anchor bolts last year. Nothing drastic, and with budget cuts and all, they elected to put off the repairs until next year. This was supposed to be a dry summer and all."

Dylan looked at the sheets of water sluicing down the front windows. The storm had grown so strong that he could no longer make out the firehouse even though it was just on the other side of Tyler Street. All the steel in the world wouldn't do any good if it didn't stay bolted to the massive concrete wall that held it in place. It was hard to imagine the water gaining that much power, but then again, was it? Hadn't he just spent an hour lashing down his boat against just such a force? Suddenly the extreme precautions didn't feel so extreme. "If that gate goes…"

"It won't be pretty. Chad went down there with a couple of other guys from public works to check it out, but who knows what they'll be able to tell in this mess?"

Dylan looked out across the room to see Karla staring at the shop entrance, visibly willing her father and Karl to walk through the door. She jumped—as did half the room— when a large crash came from the back door.

"They came in the back!" Karla said, dashing toward the delivery door at the same time Dylan turned to do the same.

It wasn't Dad and Grandpa coming through the back door. It was a ferocious surge of water. The sight sent such a jolt of fear through Karla that she had trouble pulling in a breath. "Dylan!"

He darted ahead of her and began wrestling with the door, pushing it against the wall of water that had come in when some heavy box from the back alley had been thrust against the door and knocked it open. Just the slice of outdoors she could see though the closing crack didn't look like a street at all; more like Niagara Falls. "We're flooding!" She lunged for one of the large bags of flour on the shelf behind her, grunting with the effort but determined to do whatever it took to save Karl's. She crammed it against the door once Dylan finally got it shut, then immediately reached for another one. Water was everywhere, bubbling under the door and spreading in a dark predatory puddle down the narrow hallway toward the customer tables and chairs. It felt as if the water were a living thing hunting her down.

"Pile anything you can," Dylan said after they'd shoved all the flour bags up against the door. He was soaked for what must be the fifth time, and she could hear fear in his voice for the first time. She could also hear the same fierce determination to fight back that was rising in her own chest. Karl's could not, *would not* go down on her watch. The shop was going to stay open as a haven in the storm that it had always been. She was endlessly grateful that she could see the same conviction in Dylan's eyes as they began pulling anything hefty off the pantry shelves.

"The front door is lower," she called as she began piling syrup cans atop boxes of biscuit mix, "why is it coming in here?"

"It's runoff coming down the hillside. The front door will get hit with standing water as it rises." Dylan took a short ladder used for getting items off the higher storeroom shelves and shoved it against the door that had pushed open. "This door is getting the force of the water rushing down off the dry valley slope."

He stopped for a moment, taking a quick survey of what they'd built and what was left to use. "I'll try to rig a stronger brace later. The generator is still running because I moved it up high, but once it runs out of gas, we're done. I won't be able to get out there and refuel it. For that matter, I don't even know if the gas can is still out there." He wiped his hands down his wet face. "At some point the water wins, you know?"

For a moment the back room was quieter, even though the wind buffeted the shut doors and the doomed generator still kept up its courageous surging rattle. "What are we going to do?" Karla almost didn't allow herself to ask the question, not wanting to give in to the panic it incited, but she needed to hear Dylan's answer.

He took her by the shoulders, his eyes fierce and steady, even though he was still panting from the effort of building the makeshift dam. "You and I will do everything we can." He uttered it slowly, deliberately, like a promise.

He'd said "You and I." She'd never been more grateful for such words ever. "Dylan…" She couldn't decide how to finish that sentence. *Thank you? Help me? I'm scared?* Gratitude warred with worry and fight and fear all at once. He'd smeared a smudge of dirt from his forehead down across one cheek, and she reached out to wipe the muck away from his eye.

His eyes fell closed at the touch of her fingers, and the transparent show of emotion jolted through her. It was the same connection she'd felt as they danced, but that was all about fun and this was something much deeper.

Everything boiled down to such an alarming focus. So much of what she'd thought mattered didn't really matter. Not today. Not right now.

She reached up and kissed him on his cheek. Softly, hesitantly, not even sure what she was doing or why. She felt his whole body react, heard his breath catch and his fingers tighten their grip on her shoulders. She felt him turn toward her and wait just the smallest of seconds, as if deciding whether to give in or pull away.

She knew instantly the moment he made his choice, as though the seconds—and they must have been mere seconds—stretched out far longer. Something rushed through him, something she could feel building and releasing as if—and this was the worst of all metaphors—a flood had been released. Truly, it had that much force as it washed over her and his mouth was on hers with his arms slipping around her. The power of his emotion was astoundingly strong, only with no force or danger. Instead, she felt a surge of safety and connection, as if she had found something secure to hold on to in a tidal wave of fear.

Something sloughed off her, as if she'd effortlessly shed the resistance they had both put up over days, or weeks, or probably since

that first cup of coffee. She felt herself clinging to Dylan—not out of weakness but out of
paired strength. Out of the recognition that
they were stronger together than either one
could be alone.

Suddenly all the reasons she'd given herself for keeping a distance from this man and
his world made no sense at all. They were all
facts, all still true in one sense or another,
but this—what she felt here and now—was
somehow *more* true. *Not now,* a voice in the
back of her head warned, but it was silenced
by another voice that said, *Now most of all.*
Dylan's arms tightened around her as if he'd
tasted the realization in her kiss.

The storm threw something else against
the door, startling them out of the embrace
to stare wide-eyed into each other's gaze.
Nothing had changed: Karl's was still under
threat, Dad and Grandpa were still out there
somewhere in potential danger, everything
that made Dylan an impossible choice was
still there. Only it wasn't. She was larger than
those things. God was larger and stronger than
those things, and what had just transpired in
Dylan's arms felt like the best weapon against
everything that assailed her.

She wasn't quite sure how his eyes burned
brighter, but they had doubled their inten-

sity as he looked at her and pulled in a deep breath. "I'm going to beg you to hold on to that thought for another six hours or so." How could the wonder in his eyes make her feel like laughing when the world was washing right out from under her? "Because I need to go find your grandfather."

Chapter Nineteen

She'd done something to him. Something deep and instantaneous and important that could never be undone. It vibrated through his whole body, broke his awareness wide-open and made him see things in ways he'd shut his eyes to before.

In the months since he'd bought the *High Tide*, it had come to overtake his life. He told himself that his work at the firehouse balanced out his life, but that was only on the outside. His "to do" list was balanced; his heart was not. Jesse had been right all along. He told himself he was being cautious, healing from the blow Yvonne had dealt, but he wasn't. He was hiding from life, hiding behind a boat because a hunk of wood could not betray him.

Neither could a hunk of wood love him. The *High Tide*, for all its promise and beauty, could not stretch him or heal him or challenge him in any of the ways Karla Kennedy had. The *High Tide*'s gorgeous lines would never look him in the eyes as Karla just had and show him what truly mattered.

A boat would never compel him to head out into a driving storm to find two lost men. Dylan realized, as he did the last snap on his storm gear and gave Karla's hand a final squeeze before pushing out into the rain, that he did not regret this choice one bit. A careful man might be heading out into the storm to check on his boats, but Dylan knew—down to the soles of his already-soaked shoes—that he was done being a careful man. He was ready to be a man who cared again.

As he turned into the wind and began to make his way down the street, he saw Karla place her hand on the front window of the shop. For a moment, Dylan placed his palm up to meet her hand, and watched the rain run down over his fingers as they covered the image of her hand on the other side of the glass. He would do this for her.

Water was everywhere, and deep. He didn't need a report from Jesse to guess the town's worst fears had been realized; the floodgates had failed. He couldn't see them from where he stood, but the level of water told him as surely as if he had been standing in front of the green gates as they gaped open. Trees no longer had trunks, the branches instead swaying straight out of the waterline where it had covered lower limbs. Porches now sat level with the muddy, swirling current, their steps and foundations underwater. Even peppered with raindrops as it was, Dylan knew not to trust the flat look of the surface—water that looked calm could pull an unsuspecting man off his feet in seconds.

Karla told him her father was driving a dark green sedan, so Dylan calculated the most likely route from Karl's house to the coffee shop and began to head down that street, leaning into the wind and keeping to the higher ground. For a second, he regretted not having the smaller boat, musing that in ten minutes Tyler Street would be better traveled by the *Low Tide* than by foot. Still, if God was kind, he wouldn't be out here for long. If it came to rescuing Karl and Kurt Kennedy by boat, things would have gone from bad to worse indeed.

Help me, Lord. Show me where the car is or send word that they are safe and sound.

Ten more minutes of looking only showed him that the water had crept above some porches and was now lapping at front doors.

In many parts of town, cars would no longer run and would lie stranded and waterlogged wherever they had stopped. As he turned a final corner, telling himself that he was going to need to call in the firehouse for reinforcements if Karl and Kurt were missing for much longer, he spied the orange blink of a car's hazard lights up a side street.

A dark green sedan lay angled across a dip in the road where water now collected up to the fenders. There, in the entryway of a bank, huddled two figures Dylan immediately recognized as Karl and Kurt. They were all of two blocks from the coffee shop, but a second glance registered that the older of the men was slumped against the wall and stooped in pain.

"Karl!" Dylan yelled, breaking into as fast a run as he dared on the slick cobblestone side street, "Kurt!"

"Over here!" Kurt yelled back, waving his arms. "Dad fell getting out of the car when it stuck."

Dylan peeled off his rain slicker to wrap it around the older man. "Can you walk?"

"Not well enough." Karl winced.

"I couldn't hold him up by myself. My cell phone slid out of my pocket and into the water as I tried to get him up the first time."

"Get his one arm—I'll take the other."

Together, they pulled Karl upright between the two of them, taking all his weight so that he could hobble a few steps at a time. It was laborious and slow, soaking each man to the skin as they made their way to the coffee shop's front steps, but they made it just as the water began lapping over the high Tyler Street curb outside the shop. Dylan had seen photos of Gordon Falls underwater, but he'd hoped never to take in the sorry sight with his own eyes.

"Grandpa!" Karla shouted as the three-man tangle of limbs pushed their way into the shop. "Dad! Thank goodness you're safe. What on earth happened?"

Karl looked up. "Your father hit a pothole."

Kurt Kennedy rolled his eyes. "The way the car sank, I think the tire rolled into a sewer drain with the manhole cover washed off. We must have dropped a full foot and I heard the undercarriage hit the pavement."

Together, the men eased Karl into a chair. Violet was instantly beside Karl, her hand on the old man's shoulder and her eyes shiny with thankful tears.

"I'm okay, I'm okay," he grumbled, "I just missed the curb getting out of the dumb car."

Dylan watched Kurt Kennedy catch his

daughter's eyes over the old man's head as if to say "it's a bit more serious than that."

Karla sank down onto her knees in front of her grandfather. "You're here now," she said as she mopped his soaked pants with a towel. "You're safe. And Karl's is open, Grandpa, just like it needs to be."

All the grumpiness left Karl's eyes, and he touched his granddaughter's cheek with such a tender gesture that Dylan felt his heart cinch. "That's my girl."

"You hurt your hip," Karla said in such a loving but fierce "don't you dare lie to me" tone that Dylan could only smile.

"Maybe just a little."

"Thank goodness you're here and safe now," Violet said, pressing a small kiss to the top of Karl's head. Dylan blinked. Those two really were sweet on each other. How had he gotten to a place where he forgot such wonderful things happened?

Kurt extended a hand to Dylan. "Thank you. I don't think I could have gotten him here without help."

"I'm glad I was able to find you. Karla needed to know you both were safe. We all did."

With that, Karla stood up and turned to him. "Thank you so much." She stood on her tiptoes and left an exquisitely tender kiss on his cheek. It sent such warmth through Dylan's body that he completely forgot he was soaking wet. "You're my hero."

"See!" Violet declared a little louder than Dylan would have liked, "I told you they were a pair!"

She'd never seen such a thing. Karla watched the water slowly swallow Tyler Street, watched the firemen and policemen pile sandbags up against the coffee shop door and every other shop along the street. She wiped away a tear from her eye with the back of her hand, struck again by how much she'd come to care for the place. The bored-stiff-can't-wait-to-leave attitude she'd harbored a little over a month ago seemed so misguided. Now, watching the town slowly surrender to the muddy churning water, she didn't see how she could leave it like this. Yes, Gordon Falls would come back from the disaster, but its healing would be as slow and laborious as Grandpa's.

It was late, although it had been hard to distinguish the daytime from the evening in all the dark, cold rain. Folks had settled themselves into corners and booths with the blankets brought over from the firehouse. The generator had given up hours ago, and Karl's had an oddly homey glow from the dozens of utility candles propped up in bowls and saucers on tables around the room.

Dylan had gone over to the firehouse to help with the rescue effort. Her lips still tingled from the kiss he left there before heading out the door, a lasting promise that he would return. Karla wondered again if the *High Tide* would survive the night, and what Dylan would do if his beloved boats were demolished. How does a man find the strength to start a third time?

"Pie for your thoughts," Dad said, holding a small plate with a squashed helping of blueberry pie. One of the few blessings of the evening was that with power out and the generator gone, everyone had an excuse to eat all the refrigerated and frozen desserts Karl's had before they spoiled. A girl could do worse than pie for dinner. Especially after ice cream for lunch.

Karla accepted the slice and cast her eyes beyond Dad to where Grandpa and Violet sat huddled and napping in a corner booth. "I'm wondering if it can all come back."

Dad's sigh was deep and weary. "The town? Sure it will. Gordon Falls has flooded before. People here know how to get back up and keep going."

"Why stay and do it all over again?" Karla wanted to understand the urge in her own heart. It seemed so illogical, so precious and pointless all at the same time.

"Actually, I think you can't have one without the other. The town is close-knit because of what it endures. Folks have been though a lot together." He scooped up another forkful of pie and nodded at Karl and Violet. "Did you know?"

"I suspected," Karla answered, staring at the sweet couple asleep against each other. "But I was still pretty shocked when Violet told me."

Dad shifted his weight. "I had no idea. I suppose you can't really see that kind of thing in your own father. I'm happy he's happy, though. They seem good for each other."

"He can't run Karl's anymore, can he?"

Dad blew out a long breath before he said, "No."

Karla looked at her father, his face cast in moving shadows by the rain streaming down the window. "I can."

"Well, you've certainly proven that, today especially."

Karla put down her plate. "No, I mean I can take over Karl's. I want to take over Karl's."

Dad put down his own pie. "Karla, you

don't have to put your life on hold to keep Karl's open. It's had a good run. Maybe now it's time for it to be over."

She looked around the room at the knots of people gathered together while the storm raged outside. With all the candles, it really was a sanctuary. If she sought to run a place where important things happened, Karla couldn't think of anything more important than what Karl's had done today. "No, Dad, Karl's isn't ready to close. Not on my watch."

Dad smiled. "So I guess that means it's safe to ask about Dylan? Your mom told me not to bring it up, but I think maybe the rules are different now."

She looked up at her father. "In answer to your question...yes, Dylan's part of the reason I think I want to stay."

"I suppose you can't really see that kind of thing in your own daughter," her father laughed, echoing his earlier statement. Then his eyes grew serious. "Don't make your life about what other people want from you, Karla. God calls each of us to our own lives, not by someone else's needs."

She hadn't even discussed it with Dylan yet. She'd come to the conclusion all on her own, sitting listening to the rain, listening to the quiet prayers and comforting talk of the people around her. She knew now, down to the deepest part of her soul, why Karl's stayed open in a storm. Why it had to stay open for the next storm and the one after that. Bebe would just have to hold up the Clifton without her. "No, Dad, this is all me. Well, God and me."

Her father pulled her into a long hug. She felt him turn his head toward Grandpa. "When will you tell him?"

"When the rain stops. Or we run out of pie. Whichever comes first."

Dad laughed softly. "And Dylan?"

Karla shrugged. "That's a bit harder to guess. Maybe after he finds out how his boats fared. Maybe right before. I figure God will hand me the right time."

"I'm proud of you, Karla."

Karla felt her smile spread all the way under her ribs. "I'm proud of me, too, Dad. Turns out 'Kennedys can do' after all."

Dad touched her cheek. "I never doubted it for a moment."

Chapter Twenty

"It's everywhere," Dylan said in a tired voice. It was true; mud covered every surface as Karla and Dylan walked through town surveying the damage the following morning. No matter where she looked, gray-brown muck seemed to coat every crack and crevice. Smears and clumps of grass and leaves seemed to be deposited in every corner. Even sadder still, they'd found bits and pieces of several boat decorations littered about town like discarded trash.

Dylan pointed to the building where he had told her he found Dad and Grandpa. "Look how high the water came up over there." It was frightening to consider what might have happened if Dad and Grandpa hadn't been able to move from the spot. An orange cone warned motorists of the open sewer that had swallowed Dad's tire—the manhole cover had indeed been swept away. For the hundredth time since then, Karla sent up a silent prayer of thanksgiving that everyone she loved was safe and sound. Lots of damage had been done, but no one had been seriously injured.

"And over there." Each building along Tyler Street boasted a horizontal line of silt and debris that signified the flood's high-water mark, as if the structures now boasted scars. It had turned out to be the worst flood Gordon Falls had seen in fifty years.

"They'll be able to fix that," Dylan said, pointing to the side window of Halverson's grocery store, "but I don't know about over there." He pointed to a home with a front porch that now sagged dangerously off one corner. Every intersection showed some washed-out foundation or cracked beam.

The sights pained her. She felt the town's wounds as if they were her own. Her heart had become linked to Gordon Falls. It had always been a part of her past—a pleasant memory, a welcome day trip out to see Grandpa—but something shifted the night the waters rose. Something as deep and powerful as the cascade of water that pushed through the floodgates. And, like the floodwaters, it had deposited some things while washing others away.

Dylan walked by a sorry pile of waterlogged books sitting out in front of the library where the basement had flooded. A pile of oversize papier-mâché books—float decorations, according to Violet—sat slumped and soggy beside their real-life counterparts. The sun couldn't quite make its way through the lingering clouds, giving the whole town a washed-out, low-tide kind of aura. Given how water had risen through town and then subsided, it wasn't an inaccurate description.

They'd come from the docks. Dylan had talked of the other damage they had seen in town, but had remained silent as to the fate of his boats. She'd sensed a need for space and simply stood in silent witness as he crawled over the battered boat and what was left of the dock. She didn't know if repairs were possible, couldn't guess what the state of the craft meant for Dylan, but only prayed for wisdom and comfort as he surveyed the scrapes and gashes in the *High Tide*. His beloved charter boat now listed unnaturally to one side in the water, much like the porch they had just passed.

Then, somehow gathering whatever information he needed, he had quietly turned away, taken Karla's hand, and they had walked back toward town without speaking of the *High Tide* and her future.

"What will you do?" Karla finally dared to ask.

"I don't know yet. I have insurance, but it's tough to know how this will all pan out." His voice was flat, a bit lifeless compared to his usual energy. "Fishing's out of the question for a month, maybe more."

It was hard to imagine a landlocked Dylan; the river seemed so much a part of him. "I'm so sorry."

"I am, too," he said, "and then again, not so much."

Karla looked at him, startled by the words.

"The *High Tide* had become everything to me. I used to think of that as a good thing—I was my own boss, I finally had the life I'd always denied myself, all that stuff. Only now I think she'd become too much." There was a long pause. "Here everyone thought I was taking such a huge risk with the boat, but I was actually playing it safe. It was easier to be out on the river—even with charter customers—than to be back in town with people." He turned to look at Karla. "I hid on that boat. That wasn't a river for me—it was a moat to keep everyone out."

Dylan? Charming, personable Dylan? It just went to show how cleverly a person can mask themselves and camouflage their true feelings. "You'd been hurt," she offered, squeezing his hand. "You needed something that couldn't hurt you again."

"True, but only for a while. A boat is just a boat. It's not a life. You can care for her but she can't care back, ever." He rubbed the back of his neck with his free hand, squinting up at the bleak sunlight. "I thought I'd feel awful looking over the damage. She's a pretty bad wreck at the moment. I ought to be a wreck myself."

"But…"

He stopped walking. "But I'm not. I mean, I'm sad and worried, but I'm not…devastated. I never thought I'd say this, but it's just a boat. One that either can be fixed or not. It's a thing, you know?" He pulled her just the slightest bit closer. "It's not a person or a life."

She reached up to pick a wayward strand of grass off the back of his shirt. She wanted to say a dozen things, but couldn't find a way to start any of the speeches whirring around in her head. So much of what she thought was important had shifted in the past day. Maybe it had to seep out slowly, like the way the water slowly receded, revealing what was left inches at a time.

They kept walking back toward Karl's, saying hello to people hauling debris out to the curb, stopping to help or gather updates. Time after time, folks went out of their way to thank Karla for keeping the shop open, or Dylan for rescuing Karl. More than one person lamented how sorry they were that the firehouse's anniversary celebration had been ruined—a boat parade seemed not only impossible, but silly in the face of everything else the town was facing.

Karla was hugging Jeannie Owens, whose candy shop had been flooded but thankfully not ruined, when she heard Dylan make a strange, gasping sound and then grab her by the shoulder.

She turned in the direction he tugged, and then gasped, too. Someone had taken a paintbrush to the sign in front of the coffee shop window, the one that now hung off-kilter because the bracket had been bent in the storm. Karl's Koffee had been modified—a crude addition sprawled over the original letters.

The sign now read, *Karla's Koffee*.

Karla's hand went to her chest, needing to somehow hold in the surge of emotion she now felt. "Grandpa..."

Dylan turned to look at her. "Karla?"

"I'm staying. I mean, I talked to Grandpa last night and told him I was staying, but you know Grandpa…"

His eyes took on the most amazing glow— the spark that had been missing all morning. "You're staying? You were even thinking about staying?"

"After the storm, after all that, I realized how much this place means to me. How much it means to all the people here. I can't let just anyone take over for Karl, and he needs to stop. Or at least slow down."

"Why didn't you say anything before?"

"You looked so lost down on the docks. I didn't think it was fair with all that was going through your head."

Dylan slid an arm around her waist. "Do you want to know what was going through my head? I was praying for guidance because I felt so hollow about what happened to the boats. I was wondering if God was telling me it was time to stop hiding and go back to Chicago because the only thing I hated the thought of losing—" his other hand moved up to brush against her cheek "—was you."

"Dylan…"

"I was using the river to keep people out.

Or at least at a distance. You changed that. But what changed your mind?"

Karla reached up and ran her fingers through Dylan's hair. "You." When he smiled, she added, "Well, not just you. I thought my purpose in life was to create a launching pad of sorts, a power breakfast spot where big things happened."

"Rooster's," he offered.

"I still think that, in a way. Only the storm showed me that what I really am meant to do is to create a haven. That's different than Rooster's, you know?"

Dylan looked at her. "But Rooster's was your big thing."

"The shop here is a place where a *different* kind of big thing happens. Grandpa's been doing something important, and that's why Karl's has to stay open. I know now that I'm the one to do that." She turned her head toward the edited sign. "Although I didn't ask for a name change at all—that's all Grandpa's doing."

Dylan pulled her tighter. "Maybe he knew that was just the hint you needed."

Karla planted her hands on her hips. "Well, nothing like a public announcement without asking permission, is there?"

Dylan turned her back toward him. "He's

not alone. This morning I was telling God I was ready to move back to Chicago to see if we had a shot at something because I would never ask you to stay here just for me." His hand cupped her chin. "But I think we have a real shot at something. I'm in love with you, Karla-with-a-*K*, and I am asking you to stay. I'm glad you're staying."

Everything that was missing from his spirit had returned. They belonged together; it was so easy to see. He could do more with her beside him just as she knew everything she wanted in Chicago could be right here in Gordon Falls if he was beside her. She'd spent so much time planning the perfect future when God had the best future of all right here waiting for her. "Oh, we've got a shot at something all right. That's the best announcement I've heard all day."

He ducked his face closer to hers. "Better than that sign over there?"

"How about this sign right here?" And with that she kissed him. "I love you, too. I'm staying for a hundred, reasons, but you're the best one."

Dylan leaned her back in a tango-worthy dip in reply, and gave her the sweetest, best, longest kiss the town had ever seen.

Karla knew she'd found her place in the

world. She knew Dylan would find a way to rebuild. And everyone could rest assured that "Karla's" stayed open in a storm.

Forget the enormous fish she'd landed earlier—Karla Kennedy had just landed Gordon Falls' best catch ever.

* * * * *

Dear Reader,

I've had such a grand time visiting Gordon Falls. The characters have become near and dear to me, and I've enjoyed giving them so many happy endings. If this is your first visit to Gordon Falls, I hope you will go back and read the five other books in the series: *Falling for the Fireman, The Fireman's Homecoming, The Firefighter's Match, A Heart to Heal,* and *Saved by the Fireman.* The Gordon Falls Volunteer Fire Department certainly is full of wonderful heroes with great stories to tell. The women of the Gordon Falls Community Church Knitting Circle have their own great stories, too. If you would like more information on how to start a prayer shawl ministry where you live, feel free to email me at allie@alliepleiter.com or write me at P.O. Box 7026 Villa Park, IL 60181. I love to hear from readers.

Warmly,

Questions for Discussion

1. Is there a "Karl's" where you live—a place where everyone gathers? What makes places like that so special?

2. Karla loves her family, but feels pressure from them. What pressures do you feel from your family and how have you resolved them?

3. Do you have a dream like Karla's "Rooster's"? Are you working toward that dream? If not, what's keeping you from it?

4. What breakfast food most comforts you? Do you have a favorite family recipe?

5. Have you ever had your heart broken like Dylan? What helped you heal? What scars remain?

6. Is there an Oscar Halverson in your community? What hurts drive people to be grumpy like that? What can you do to help them?

7. Dylan loves his boats—perhaps a bit too much. Is there something in your life you are in danger of loving too much?

8. If Violet showed up at your door ready to "kidnap" you onto a fishing trip, would you go? Why or why not?

9. What is your "haven in a storm"? Could you be one for others?

10. Have you ever been faced with a choice like Karla's between Perk and Karl's? What did you choose? Do you have any regrets?

11. Is there a time in your life where God's plans were so different—yet so much better—than your own?

12. How does a disaster like Gordon Falls' flood build a community? How can it harm a community? If you know of a town facing disaster, how can you pray for them today?

LARGER-PRINT BOOKS!

GET 2 FREE LARGER-PRINT NOVELS PLUS 2 FREE MYSTERY GIFTS

Love Inspired®

SUSPENSE
RIVETING INSPIRATIONAL ROMANCE

Larger-print novels are now available...

ReaderService.com

Manage your account online!

- Review your order history
- Manage your payments
- Update your address

> *We've designed
> the Harlequin® Reader Service
> website just for you.*

Enjoy all the features!

- Reader excerpts from any series
- Respond to mailings and
  special monthly offers
- Discover new series available to you
- Browse the Bonus Bucks catalog
- Share your feedback

Visit us at:
ReaderService.com